GREEN
INFERNO
THE WORLD CELEBRATES YOUR DEMISE
I0746711

GREEN INFERNO
THE WORLD CELEBRATES YOUR DEMISE

GREEN INFERNO

THE WORLD CELEBRATES YOUR DEMISE

AN ANTHOLOGY OF TERRESTRIAL HORROR

EDITED BY
MATT BLAIRSTONE

FOR RAMONE

*Though the pieces we leave you seem damaged beyond repair,
I know you will build something magnificent from them.*

CONTENTS

TENEBROUS TIDINGS

It could have been the COVID-19 pandemic; I mean, in a sense, every domino that fell in 2020 was related to that devastation.

It could have been the crashing waves of racial injustice, authoritarian brutality and incompetence, and the righteous rage that consumed the United States.

It could have been the political upheaval and lies and divisiveness that seemed (seems?) neverending.

But in the end, the singular episode that laid the foundation for Tenebrous Press and *Green Inferno* was a September morning spent navigating a barren stretch of coastal highway in the midst of the worst wildfires in Oregon's history; my wife at the wheel, my son in the backseat, and me blindly guessing at a direction that would lead us away from the looming blazes and not steer us directly into its heart. The briny ocean air--one of my favorite things about living near the coast-- replaced by something noxious and torrid that coated our throats and weighed tangibly on our skin.

We made it out, obviously; but the sky's sickly yellow-gray pallor followed us back to Portland and enveloped the city, and most of the Pacific Northwest, in a weeklong blanket of ash and gloom. I had never realized how much I take for granted something so innocuous as opening a window and breathing fresh air... how blessedly entitled I am to have a window to close in the first place...to have a house at all, and the ability to close off this mad world for stretches at a time.

(It says something about the state of current affairs that by the time we arrived home, QAnon wingnuts were already spreading the "news" that these fires were intentionally lit by, ahem, "antifa activists", and were *absolutely not of course not no way* the result of our dire state of climate crisis, *don't be ridiculous with your wackadoo science ya leftist commie.* If I took the time to share my thoughts on that particular line of insanity, we'd never get to the bloody heart of this book!)

...But I digress. Anyway: that was September 2020. By October, my vision for an anthology collecting the horror stories of creators from across the globe, exploring their connections to--and thoughts on--this chaotic, angry world had begun to crystallize; and in November I cast my net to snare as many Horror kids, creeps and weirdos as I could fit into this inaugural volume.

From there, the Tenebrous family tree blossomed...or festered, maybe.

If something positive can come from a year-plus of pandemic-related strife and turmoil, I hope it's that the creative spirits of the world can shake free of the chains that have existed for far too long, that force us to hew to the path of *how it's always been done*. There is no model anymore. Smash it. Build something new, something better.

I'm a middle-aged man playing a young game, but I've got a lifetime's worth of Horror fandom to draw from. I'm not looking to replicate the past, but if I can give you a twinge of the chills I felt the first time I read Caitlin R. Kiernan or Jack Ketchum or Poppy Z. Brite...Alan Moore's *Swamp Thing* or Charles Burns' *Black Hole* or the heyday of Vertigo Comics (R.I.P.)...Shirley Jackson, Splatterpunk, the *Borderlands* anthology, Thomas Ligotti, *The Ballad of Black* Fucking *Tom*...then I'll have done my job.

This volume, with its unwieldy title--*Green Inferno: The World Celebrates Your Demise*--is Tenebrous Press' opening cannonade, our mission statement, our mix-tape. This is a sampling of what you can expect to see from this little publishing entity in the months and years to come: terrifying stories both short and long, from creators around the world. Comics (and *Comix*) that smash Pop-sheen scares and Pulp greasiness together. It's a big world; there's a lot of scary shit out there, and infinite ways to frighten folks.

If you're a fan and devourer of flesh-crawling fiction and comics, we want to hear from you! We want to know what you think is lacking in the Horror marketplace, what you want to see more of, what works, what doesn't work.

If you are a creator, we invite you to get in touch as well! We want to give voice to Horror artists and writers who perhaps haven't had the opportunity to get their voices heard. Tell me your craziest outside-the-box ideas; I want to hear 'em!

You can reach us at tenebrouspress@gmail.com. At the moment "we" are just "me", but rest assured I'll respond. Tenebrous has a lot of Horror in store for you. I can't wait to share my stories, and those of countless other creators, with you.

Hail Indie Horror! Welcome to the Inferno.

Matt Blairstone
Publisher, Tenebrous Press
Editor, *Green Inferno*
Portland OR, May 2021

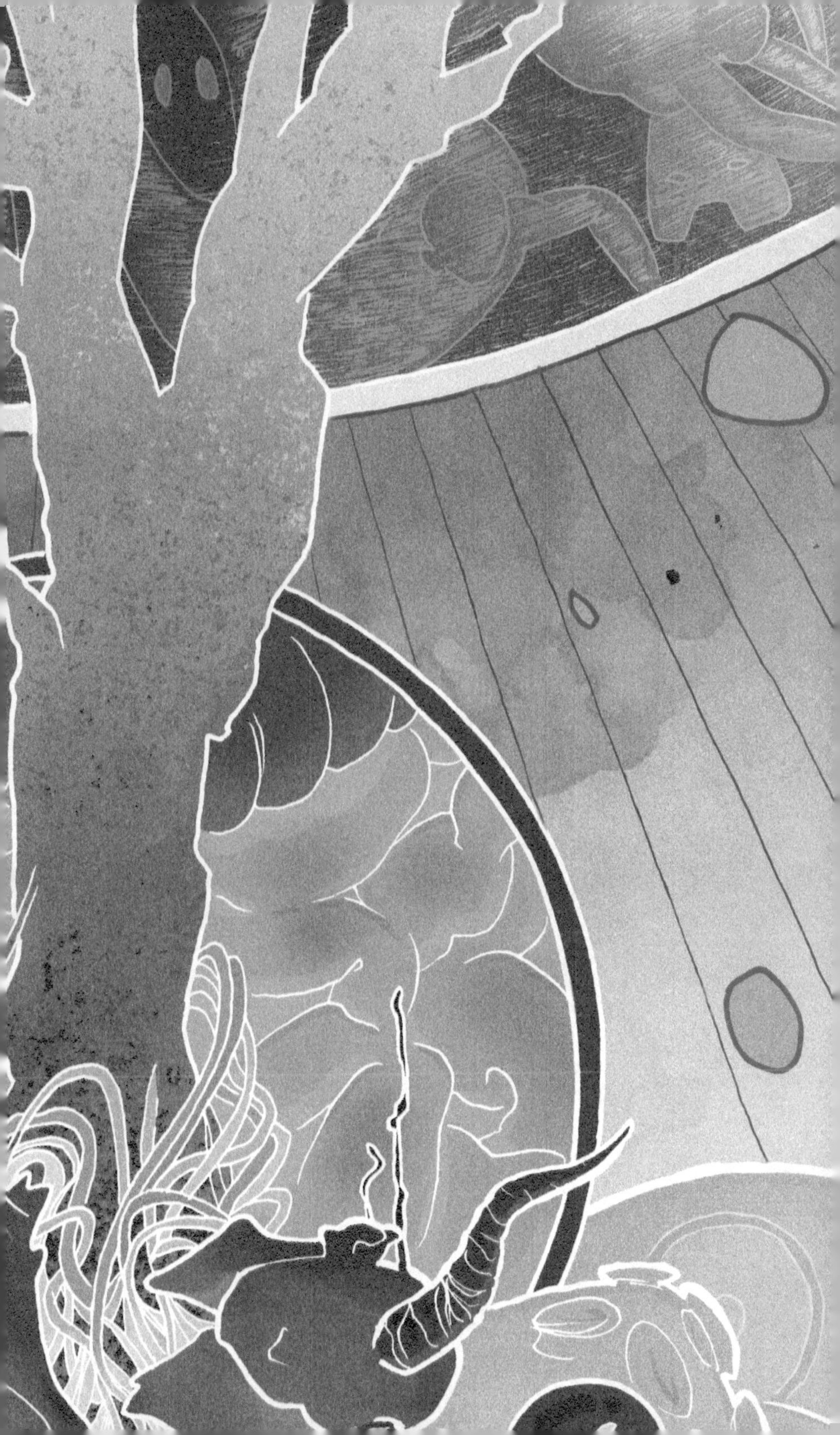

My first brush with horror was a one-two punch of *Alien*
and *The Omen*. I saw those both when I was *very* young
and they terrified me in the best way. I became a
horror fiend and gorehound by the time I was eight...
seeking out the scariest, weirdest, bloodiest
horror I could find, in whatever medium.

I am, unsurprisingly, something of a fatalist. We're
well past the point of no return with our abuse of the planet.
I know the Earth will continue well beyond our time here
and will recover from our damage quite swiftly...but we are
poisoning our own world against ourselves.

Blacky Shepherd

INVERSUS

Bobby Bermea

There's not a time in my life that I recall not
liking ghosts and monsters and the like.
I loved *Scooby Doo* except for one thing:
the ghosts were never real. I hated that.

I've not yet cracked the code with horror in theatre.
There's a unique opportunity there to immerse the
audience in something awful but it's hard to achieve
as much visually as film...it's a tough nut to crack.

Earth was around for a couple billion years before
we got here and will be for another couple billion
afterwards. All art--all of it--is essentially a scream
into the void that we are still here, that we matter.
But we don't.

Denied her rightful tribute, the Scum Queen, seething and starved, turned her attention to the inferior offering left her.

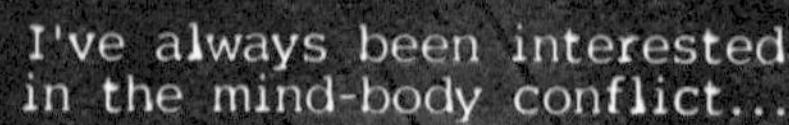
I've always been interested
in the mind-body conflict...

...how the mind sometimes fails
to acknowledge the body's limitations...

Lena Ng

THE CALL OF THE CAVE DWELLER

...the power of belief, and how the body
doesn't always bend to those beliefs...

...No matter how often you try to warn people...
SOME JUST NEED TO LEARN THE HARD WAY.

THE CALL OF THE CAVE DWELLER
BY LENA NG

Time will pass as it always does. Warnings and reports will be forgotten. The primordial deity slumbered in the depths of the savage seas. The warning sign at the mouth of its ocean abode could no more forewarn the reader than to scream in his ear.

STOP

PREVENT YOUR DEATH!

GO NO FURTHER.

FACT: You need cave training & cave equipment to cave dive.

FACT: Over 300 divers have died in caves just like this.

FACT: It CAN happen to YOU!

There's nothing in this cave worth dying for!

DO NOT GO BEYOND THIS POINT.

But all this—the dark, mysterious, bowel-like tunnels, which were barely the width of a coffin; the absence of sound except for the deep inhuman breathing through the respirator; the somber water, and the oddness and frightfulness of a sign in the middle of the dark blue sinkhole, illustrated by a hooded grim reaper holding a scythe—held no alarm for the man nor his son. They had always been, and would always be, the types to take a warning as a challenge.

A leathery diver had said no one could pay him enough to go on this dive. How that diver had scoffed at him! At the time the man knew enough of diving to boast, but not enough to realize, this dive was well above his ability and training. He mistook new equipment as a substitute for skill. Now, with the intimidating blackness in front of him, the man finally had a small inkling of the danger.

The man and his son understood the sign's words but not their significance; death was only something which could happen to other people. They were immortal and invulnerable, with no fear of the fragility and powerlessness which comes with disability. To them, the spirit would always conquer the body and its inconsequential needs.

To the man and his son, diving ninety metres below the ocean's surface into an unmapped maze of dark and narrow tunnels with a limited supply of oxygen meant checking off another item on a bucket list. It meant bragging rights on Facebook and pictures on Instagram. It meant collecting followers and 'Likes,' building an audience, building a brand, building a channel on YouTube.

The sign did not cause them to reflect upon their vulnerable dependence on air, as terrestrial creatures who can only live within ranges of oxygen levels, and it did not cause them to reflect upon their infinitesimal hiccough of existence. Death could be evaded by the use of neoprene suits, flippers, oxygen canisters, depth readers, and buoyancy control devices. They could thumb their noses at the hooded, skeletal figure who lurked in the murky ocean and resurface triumphant.

Despite his lack of survival sense, the man knew that his supply of oxygen, like his life in an abstract fashion, was limited. The adventure must be completed within the time dictated by the air canister. To avoid getting lost, a guide line had been tied to the base of the warning sign. Besides, the claustrophobic darkness of the tunnels had ignited a spark of alarm; the man began to look forward to drinking a cold ale in a warm pub, bragging to his pedestrian friends, clapping a hand on the shoulder of his admiring son. He pulled on the line to follow it to the exit. To his dismay, the line tightened, snapped, then turned slack. He pulled the rope until at last he held up a frayed end. The line had rubbed on a sharp tooth of limestone.

Without his guide line, the man had only his poor intuition to rely upon. At one tunnel, he pulled himself out in panic. None of these things he could tell his son in the deep silent pressure of the ocean's fold; his son could only follow, the faithful innocent led astray by a false prophet.

Despite all the admonitions not to do this when in a dangerous situation, no one can control panic. The cave's tunnels had a terrifying sameness, orienting themselves anywhere but to the water's surface. The man followed a hairpin turn. He realized his mistake early but his faithful son blocked the exit. He moved deeper into the trap until he was wedged in so tightly he could neither move forward nor back. His son tried pulling and tugging. He then tried pushing and shoving. All the while, the air ran down like a deadly timer.

As the men struggled, their movements awakened the slumbering god. Like a Venus flytrap stimulated by movement on its sensor hairs, by instinct the intestinal tunnel walls which encased the men tightened and undulated; peristalsis drew them deeper into the earth's gullet. The men desperately tried to free themselves from their chosen watery tomb. They squandered their diminishing life force by thrashing about; the deity took this as an offering. It fed until the men stopped moving.

When escaping air bubbles no longer tickled its limestone entrails, the intestinal tunnels relaxed, regurgitating the remains as a snake regurgitates bones. Together in life, together in death, father and son floated side-by-side in the silent waters.

A day later, three wise men in neoprene suits with oxygen canisters removed the waste. The claw marks on the tunnel walls would be interpreted by future historians as indecipherable words of scripture. As one, the priestly divers bowed their heads, touched their foreheads and chests, and gave thanks. The sacrificial few had given up their lives to save the many. Satiated, the primordial deity returned to its malignant slumber. Someday it would fully awaken and its followers would rejoice in terror at the coming of a new Dark Age.

Time will pass as it always does. Warnings and reports will be forgotten. The incomprehensible cave horror bides its time, engorging itself on the endless feast of man's folly.

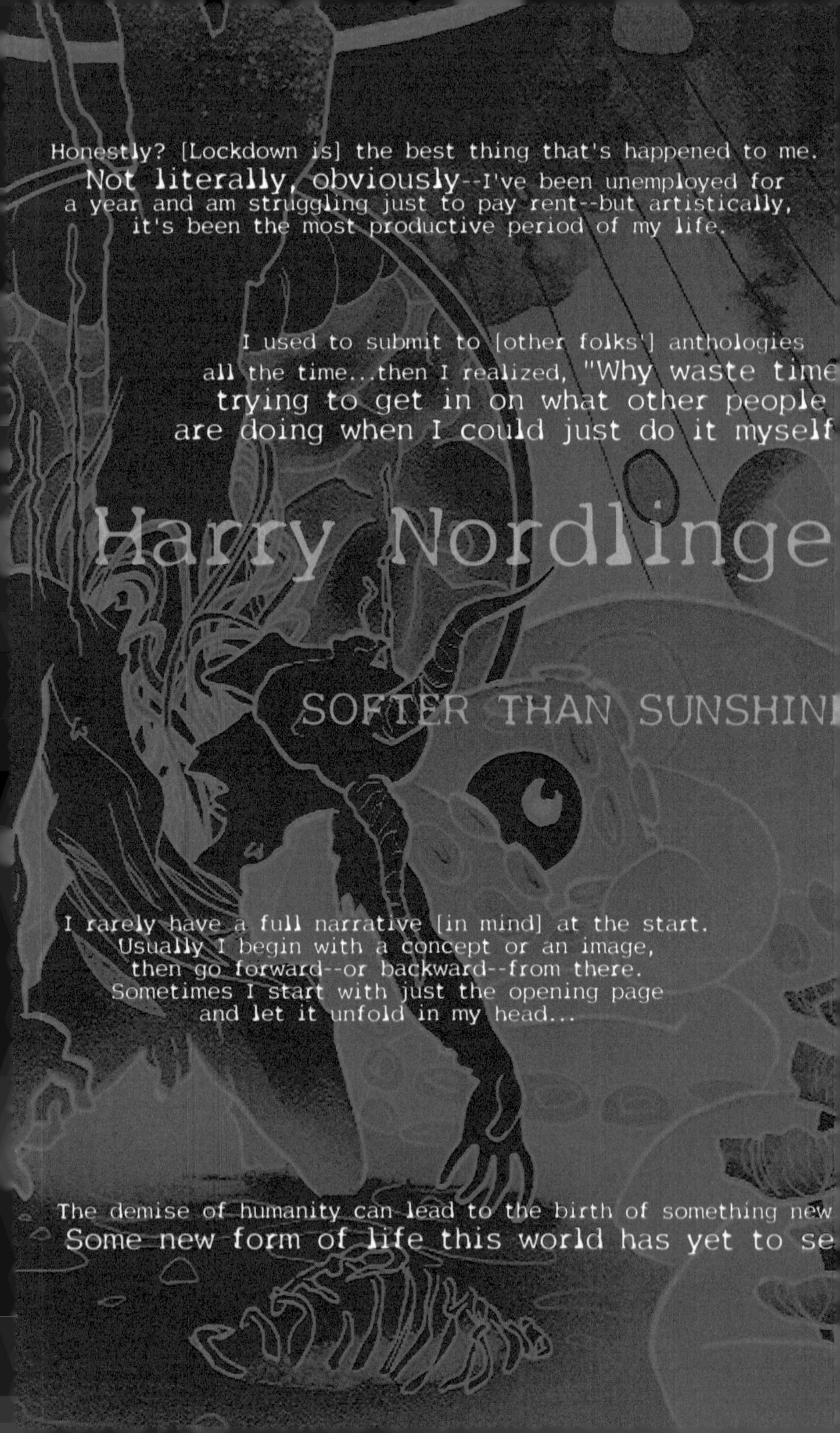

Honestly? [Lockdown is] the best thing that's happened to me.
Not literally, obviously--I've been unemployed for
a year and am struggling just to pay rent--but artistically,
it's been the most productive period of my life.

I used to submit to [other folks'] anthologies
all the time...then I realized, "Why waste time
trying to get in on what other people
are doing when I could just do it myself

Harry Nordlinge

SOFTER THAN SUNSHIN

I rarely have a full narrative [in mind] at the start.
Usually I begin with a concept or an image,
then go forward--or backward--from there.
Sometimes I start with just the opening page
and let it unfold in my head...

The demise of humanity can lead to the birth of something new
Some new form of life this world has yet to se

GREEN INFERNO

OH.

SQUIG

SQUIGGLE

THERE YOU
ARE.

THWACK!!

NOW LET'S GO
FIND MARSHA!

I draw a fair amount of inspiration
from the great unknowns of nature.

No specific event in my life inspired this story,
just a clear sense that nature is completely amoral
and utterly neutral; whether we as a species
live or die has no bearing on the world.

Erica Ruppert

UNDERNEATH

Life appears in surprising and aggressive forms;
humans, despite their cunning, are just animals and
not always the fittest for survival.

UNDERNEATH
BY ERICA RUPPERT

The winter's cold lasted deep into April, and the muddy snow was slow to retreat.

At last, though, it had let go, and now the sharp wind carried the scent of damp earth. Above, the sun was a white glare in a pale blue sky. Elena leaned against the door frame, squinting into the light.

She looked over the wet porch and the scattered bodies the melting snow had laid bare. Small things, wet and soft and mangled, unwanted and left by the feral cats. She prodded the corpse of a squirrel with her toe. Its fur clung to her shoe as she pulled her foot away.

She had hoped spring would bring a return, a renewal. But no birds sang in the bright still air, no living small bodies rustled among the dried stems and new shoots.

Underneath

Elena shook her head as she swept the detritus of a thousand tiny lives from her porch. She remembered when her pet cats had still been alive and would leave dead mice for her on the doorstep. One time they brought her the chipmunk that lived in the stone wall that bordered the front of the cabin, the one she had taught to take peanuts from her hand. Now only the ferals remained, skittish and predatory.

But that wasn't right, she thought. She had misremembered. Elena had not seen any cats at all over winter, or any of their neat tracks in the snow. Not for a few years, now. The cats were all long gone; her pets, and the wild ones as well.

Maybe the litter of small, dead things was the price of some new instinct awakened by the clinging cold. Maybe they had tried to get inside, had died seeking shelter.

She was lonely. She might have welcomed them.

***

Aaron had died three years ago. Before the birds were gone, but after the cats. The world was getting smaller. Elena wondered what else she would outlive.

Their retreat to the vacation cabin had seemed a wise idea, years ago when the blight and its rot had begun to empty the cities. Aaron had borrowed a van and packed it with books, seeds and hand tools, and drove them far from the thinning crowds to their familiar getaway.

It had been idyllic at first. They had turned the wide yard into a garden, beaten back the enclosing woods, and hidden from the failing world. No one came to the other cabins in the enclave. It was only them and the cats. Once they ventured down to the tiny general store near the main road, but it was locked up and abandoned. Feeling like thieves, they broke a window and took all the packaged food they could find. Just in case.

For the first few years the ground they prepared and planted had been fertile enough. But by the time Aaron fell ill the harvest had declined to barely enough. Elena was cautious about their diminishing stores. She foraged, with a book on edible wild plants stuck in her pocket. She learned the tastes of acorns, of wild fruits, of twining roots. She learned to live with a certain level of hunger.

The garden flourished again after Aaron had finally wasted away at the end of a cold March. After she had buried what was left of him at what had once been the edge of the property, when there were such boundaries. It was as if the garden had waited for him.

***

Pale roots scrawled across the cellar walls like cobwebs. She kept away from the walls when she went down there to bring up what was left.

The vegetables and hard-shelled squash she had stored in the cellar were turning to slime, kept far past their time. She cut away the worst parts of the potatoes and onions and boiled what was left for her breakfast.

She had started her seeds a few weeks ago; early, given the weather. But she was anxious for fresh food. The trays lined the southern window sills, delicate sprouts pushing up and toward the light.

Every day the young plants were taller, leaning into the sun, anchored by burgeoning roots. They seemed alien to her. Hungry. Wanting. She shuddered. She had thought about them too much.

***

Despite the morning chill she brought the trays of tender seedlings out onto the damp porch. She knew there would probably be another frost before spring truly took hold, but she couldn't stand to have them in the cabin any longer, to hear them stretch and strain toward the sun. The cold frame would keep them warm enough.

The day was clear as glass, the bare trees like a lattice around her. She thought she might as well check the garden plot and begin clearing it for the coming crops. She marched down the two porch steps and over the thawing ground, feeling it give beneath her boots. The stone path to the back of the house was slick with decaying leaves, and she slowed her pace as she headed for the tool shed.

As she turned the corner she saw the tarp had slipped off the woodpile as the melting snow shifted its weight. Much of the wood was wet. She stopped short, all at once unsure of when she had last been back here. Surely she had brought in firewood only a day or two ago. Surely she would have noticed the tarp.

Maybe she had forgotten her task midway through it? She marvelled at her own confusion, but pushed this thought away. Instead she opted to fill the waiting cart and lug it over the rutted, softening ground to the back of the cabin. She hoped there was still enough dry wood inside for later. Then she returned to the shed for the spade, fork, and hand tools, and crossed the muddy yard to the wide garden clearing.

The fence was still in good shape, the wire still bright, the posts still straight. Last year's vines tied the gate shut, though; the brown, brittle stems twined like knots through the hinges. She tugged, harder than she thought she would have to, and the dry stems crackled and broke apart. The gate dragged a furrow across the thawing earth. She smelled mud.

As she entered the garden, Elena looked more closely at the mess of bleached stems that littered the ground. Tangled among them were the small round skulls of squirrels and other rodents. She could tell by the teeth.

She mourned their deaths but moved forward. She had to make the ground ready. Bones snapped like twigs beneath her feet. Above her, the sky was nearly white.

She dug her spade into the soil. It felt too wet, like sticky dough. A bubble of grey-green slime pushed up through the broken crust. Dark lines swirled through the curve of it, like veins beneath a membrane. She squinted at it, wondering what had caused it. Then the bubble burst in upon itself.

As if that had been a release, thin green tendrils threaded suddenly up through the cold ground, carrying bones and feathers with them.

They grew as she watched, stretching toward the bright, weak sun, snaking around her boots. She jumped away from their clinging progress, surprised at how much effort it took to tear them off. She grabbed at her tools, strode out of the garden and shut the gate behind her. She could hear the vines slithering along the ground as she headed back to the cabin.

It was her imagination, she told herself. She was hungry and lonely. She was letting her fears get ahead of her. She struggled not to cry. If she cried, she would never stop.

She stood perfectly still for a long moment, collecting herself. She did not hear the plants growing. She would not hear them. She kept her back to the garden.

She picked up the trays of seedlings and dropped them under the cold frame. Before she closed the glass top she bent down and pried one tiny plant from its cell. She imagined she felt its fine roots move against her palm. She closed her fingers around it to trap them in place as she walked to what was, for her, the edge of the property.

She raked away the wet black leaves that covered Aaron's grave like a dirty sheet. His unmarked stone glistened with the trails of slugs. The dark earth over him was riddled with tiny white roots, the plants they had once supported dried up and broken away. She scuffed her boot over the damp ground. Aaron was under there, feeding the new growth that would come.

She hadn't thought of it like that when she had buried him.

Kneeling, she broke the crust of the soil with a trowel and scooped out a hole for the fragile seedling. A thick liquid bubbled up from the bottom of the shallow hole, easing over the edge and seeping into the surrounding ground. It was darker than the slime in the garden. *Syrupy.*

Elena jumped back, horrified that she had sunk the trowel blade into Aaron's remains. But it wasn't possible. It had been too long. There would be nothing of him left.

She peered into the hole. The liquid had receded like a wave from the shore, pooling at the very bottom. It smelled of decaying vegetation, not meat. She gently prodded the soil with the tip of the blade. The liquid clung in a greasy, iridescent slick on the pitted steel.

It must be the groundwater, she thought, high from the melting snow and contaminated with the sludge of last year's plants.

She dropped the single seedling into the hole. As she patted the soil down around it, she felt the earth sink beneath her hands, as if something pulled it from below.

***

The sun still shone, but Elena could not be outside any longer. She needed to eat something, and calm herself. She thought there were still a few tea bags tucked away in the cabinet. She would finish clearing up the garden tomorrow.

She scraped the mud from her boots and left them with her gardening gloves on the porch. Smears still followed her into the house, inescapable. She had never gotten used to the tenacity of it, the way dirt would find a way in.

As she wiped the floor clean she saw the mud had worked its way under her fingernails and into the seams of her hands, despite the gloves. She picked at the dirt beneath her nails. Bits of root came out with faint snaps.

Before they had fled, before the blight, she had enjoyed gardening. How long ago was that, now? How long since they had fled?

As she washed her hands she felt dizzy. Her throat felt hot, swollen.

If she were getting sick she could excuse her imaginings. She could recover.

She took the small mirror from the wall and brought it to a window to examine herself.

The skin on her jaw and neck had turned a ghastly violet, as if a huge bruise had spread over her throat. Elena pressed her fingers into it. Her flesh felt soft, overripe. Skin sagged beneath her eyes, exposing the mottled grey meat beneath it. Rivulets of grey-green fluid trickled across the revealed flesh like falling tears. There was no pain, just a strange heaviness.

It had to be her imagination. She was so tired.

She placed the mirror on the sill and leaned toward it.

She tugged gently, and felt her face slip down. Loose skin slid over her eyes like a hood. She felt streams of thin liquid flow down her face, abruptly released. She felt scattered points of sharp pressure in the liquid's wake, as what had been hidden beneath the shroud of her skin pushed out, like seedlings, like young sprouts, reaching for the light.

Elena dug her fingers into her sliding skin and pulled, suddenly curious, suddenly eager. Her face felt like the wet, sucking earth.

She wondered what was blooming underneath.

Diane Barker

Harrison Webb

UPROOTED

I've lived in Portland for over ten years now.
The climate has changed rapidly. We used to have
mild weather with snowstorms every [few] years...
Now, the temperatures are chaotic.
We never needed air conditioning before;
now facing a summer without one is daunting.

My friends and I joke about how California has "fire season"
as part of its yearly cycle... but in all seriousness,
the fires worsen [every] year as climate conditions
exacerbate the frequent droughts and dry out the foliage.

...I feel more at home in a forest than in the urban jungle.
As such, I'm sympathetic to the idea of nature fighting back
against humans that wish to subdue or destroy it.

It doesn't matter how big your wallet is.
nature, the climate, the planet?
They don't give a fuck.

UPROOTED

DIANE BARKER & HARRISON WEBB

EXCEPT FOR *THIS*, CHARITY.
THE *COUNCIL* SAID WE CAN'T *KNOCK IT DOWN*.

ACCIDENTS *HAPPEN* IN CONSTRUCTION *ALL THE TIME*.

THEY WON'T BE HAPPY...
PFFT! SO WE'LL APOLOGISE AND MAKE A HEFTY DONATION TO THE *LOCAL YOUTH CLUB* OR WHATEVER.
IT'LL BE *FIIINE*.

NOT A GOOD IDEA TO PISS OFF THE LOCALS TWO SECONDS AFTER GETTING HERE.
GROW A FUCKING PAIR, TODD. IT'S JUST A GODDAMN TREE.

SOON...

CRRRAAAASSSSHH--
LOOK OUT!

NATURE SENT MANY WARNINGS...

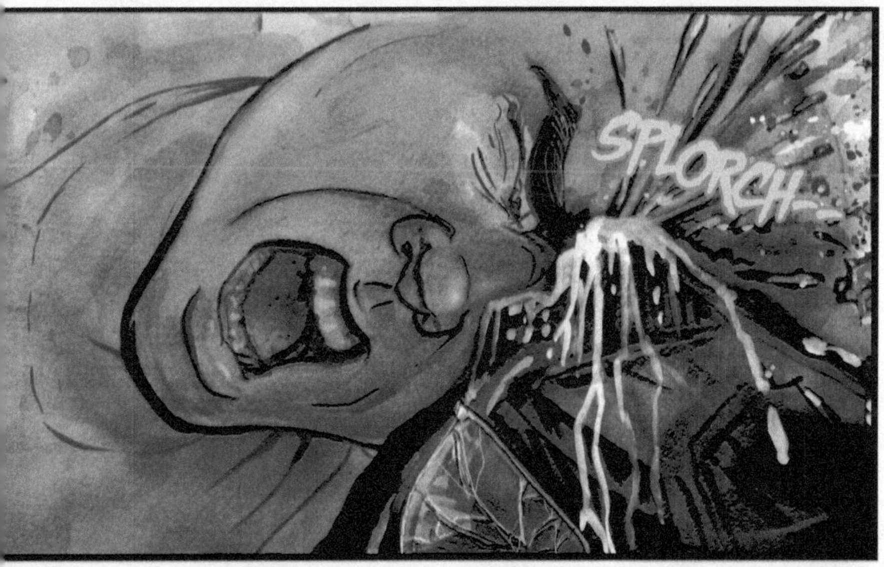

SPLORCH

I'VE LOST THREE MEN TO THIS FUCKING JOB! WE ARE DONE!
THOSE WERE ACCIDENTS, YOU SUPERSTITIOUS SHIT!

FUCK YOU, TODD! FIND SOMEONE ELSE. I'M KEEPING MY BOYS SAFE.

YOU'RE GONNA REGRET THIS, DAVE! I WILL SUE THE SHIT OUTTA YOU!

...BUT TODD AND CHARITY REFUSED TO LISTEN.
HOW MANY IS THAT NOW?!
FOUR CONTRACTORS. THIRTEEN DEATHS. MAYBE THIS WAS A BAD IDEA...?

NO. THIS IS MY DREAM HOUSE. YOU WILL FINISH THIS...

...I DON'T CARE HOW MUCH BLOOD IT TAKES.

TWO WEEKS LATER.
TODD--!

...

NOOOOOO--!

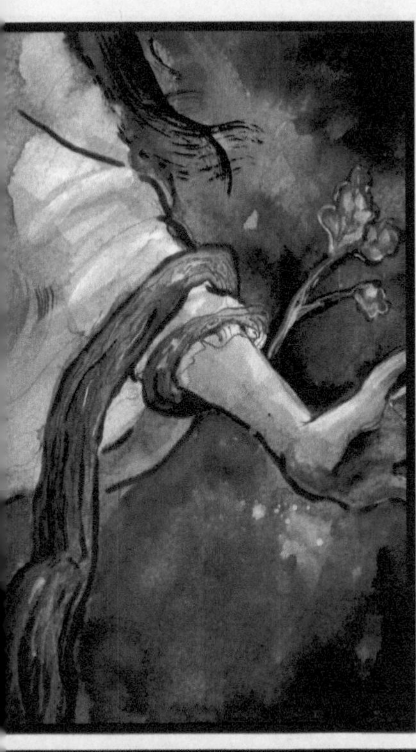

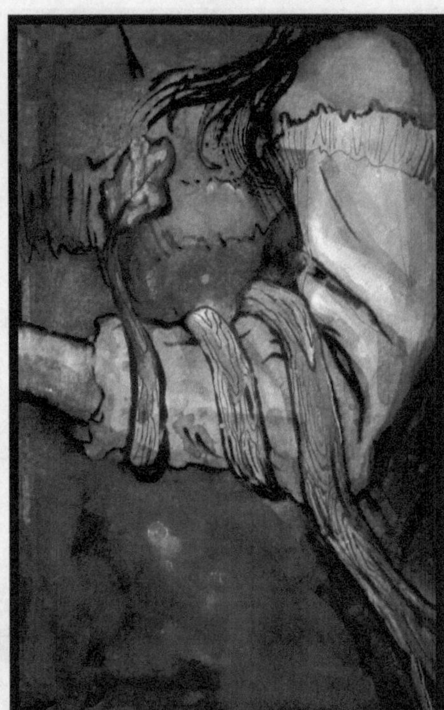

GAHHH--!
SHRRIIIPPP--

SOME PLACES ARE NOT MEANT FOR US...
AND THEY NEVER WILL BE.
END.

...I tend to veer from stories
that are too morally black and white...

...I do have a somewhat adventurous palette...
as long as [we're talking] interesting spices...

Lorna D. Keach

A STRANGE FINCH

...The things [that the Protagonist] loves he
consumes...his most recent acquisition
gives him precisely what he wants...
AND THEN SOME.

A STRANGE FINCH
BY LORNA D. KEACH

It was the night of the dinner party, and Zachary Vautour snuck into the kitchen in hopes of stealing a taste.

On the menu that evening was braised California condor in truffle sauce with an amuse-bouche starter of kakapo tempura. Sadly, it wasn't among what he felt were his most interesting selections. Although Vautour was fascinated by the small pink chunks of kakapo the chef tossed with oil, he'd already eaten condor during his last dinner party and found it to be lacking in flavor. But the kakapo wouldn't make for a main course on its own. The plump little nuggets of flesh were so tiny, he could hardly call them a snack.

He stood over the left shoulder of his chef and plucked one chunk of kakapo out of the bowl. The chef set her tongs down with a clatter and, huffing, waited for Vautour's long arm to leave her personal space. After he'd snatched up a morsel, he took a step back and popped it in his mouth. His chef had tried to stop him eating raw poultry before, a habit he picked up overseas, but Vautour had convinced her any arguments about the health implications were useless. He loved a good *pate*. He loved strange meat. He loved the creatures his suppliers smuggled in live with their glistening feathers and banshee shrieking. (He heard their exotic songs even from the kitchen, cries radiating from the lower levels of the estate in his "aviary" several hundred feet below ground, where he'd tucked away the endangered rarities to keep all to himself). The things Zachary Vautour loved, he always put in his mouth. He wanted them *inside* him, as complete a capture as possible.

He closed his lips around the Kakapo and breathed, inhaling its coppery scent, letting its raw, thin blood dribble down his tonsils.

***

That evening, his supplier delivered a shipment at a most opportune time. "Amazing, Falke. Simply amazing." Vautour clapped the man on the back. "You'll stay for dinner and tell us all about your adventure, yes?"

"Sure," Falke said, "Hope you've got the stomach for it. It was grisly."

"Hah! That just whets my palate."

At the table, Falke cut a charming, roguish figure among Vautour's well-dressed friends; the man wore the soot-stained camp shirt he stumbled in with, his sandy hair tousled from the drive. He'd had to complete the delivery himself after some trouble with the expedition vessel, so he was eager to take part in refreshments. "At least I didn't have to suffer through customs!" Falke laughed.

Vautour ordered the staff to bring out the crate Falke had delivered; now emptied, of course. The guests marveled at the GALAPAGOS stamped in aggressive capital letters along the lid. They insisted they see the new arrivals to Vautour's aviary.

As they all stood up and made their way downstairs to view the cages, the chef hovered by the kitchen door, glaring, her kakapo tempura quickly losing its flavor.

***

Down below, in a wire-and-steel enclosure beside the Spix's macaw and the dwarf cassowary, was a goose-looking bird with a white breast, brown wings, and webbed feet the color of the sky.

"The *Galápagos blue-footed booby*," Vautour announced. He knew he should have kept his acquisition a secret to capitalize on the element of surprise for his guests, but the next two events were planned for the cassowary and the macaw, and he couldn't contain his urge to brag.

When one guest commented that boobies were relatively prolific in South America, Vautour huffed that any chump could not just waltz in and grab something off Darwin Island. He demanded Falke "tell them how tough it was."

Falke shrugged. "I got Russians to do it." The guests nodded knowingly.

Vautour, while conversation distracted the others, reached his thick white fingers through the booby's enclosure and plucked out a small tuft of feather. He placed it in his mouth; the rancid odor rose up his nasal cavity, the dry fluff sank into his tongue like a salty cotton candy. He imagined the infinitesimal mites inside it squirming against the landscape of his taste buds.

His guests, however, paid no notice to Vautour's unhygienic nibble, as someone pointed out a nearby enclosure with another new arrival to the edible collection. Vautour was at a loss; he'd never seen the thing before either.

"Oh, that thing," Falke muttered. "It was a stowaway." The bird inside the cage was similar to a sparrow or a songbird—*finch-like*—with dark feathers and a heavy beak down-turned in a scowl. It blinked eyes like tiny cold marbles in a broad head.

"He looks like he sucked a lemon!" One guest commented.

"He sucked something," Falke said. "I found him attached to the booby."

The guests erupted in laughter at that, Vautour included.

Falke nodded, smiled, went along with the joke until the tittering stopped, whereupon he said, "The little guy was on the booby's tail feathers, pecking the shit out of him and slurping up the blood. The Russians said some finches on the island did that when water was hard to find. Turned to blood-drinkers."

The guests' laughter died down.

"This guy was different though. Hungrier," Falke said. "When I caught him he looked about ready to stick his entire head in and eat the booby from the inside." He kept his tone jovial. "The booby didn't even notice it was there. It was too stupid—or numb—to see it was being eaten. Maybe this finch has got weird enzymes in its spit or something. Sure is a greedy little vampire fuck, though. I could barely pull him off."

Silence followed.

Vautour broke it by saying, "I imagine vampire birds taste excellent. Extra gamey!"

The joke livened things up. Bright faces and conversation returned to his guests, and they fluttered with smiles and laughter before moving upstairs to take part in a now-soggy tempura. Vautour would, of course, blame the sogginess on the fact he'd hired a *three*-star chef.

As they left the aviary, Vautour heard creaking, as if the enclosure wire strained against a substantial force. He paid it no mind. The cassowary was a real prick, but so far its cage had held.

***

While heaping great forkfuls of condor into their mouths, glistening lips shining beneath the track lighting of the formal dining room, conversation again turned to the booby downstairs, with one guest asking

Falke if the Russians gave him much trouble.

Falke shook his head. "The Russians had the trouble themselves."

The *Krasnaya Ptitsa*—the expedition vessel he'd commissioned to smuggle the birds off Galápagos—had ended its "scientific mission" drifting lifeless off the coast of Portoviejo; a minor international incident for the Ecuadorians. If it hadn't been for Falke's contacts, the contents of the ship would still be under lockdown and he'd never have gotten the birds out of the country. Investigators suspected smugglers out of Hong Kong. The entire crew, Falke explained, had been murdered.

"Details, man," Vautour said. "Give us the gory details."

Falke didn't know much beyond that, apart from the fact his contacts told him the crew's backs had been broken--demolished, really--as if someone had taken a pickaxe to their lumbar areas and chipped away a huge bloody hole.

"I've never heard of the Chinese doing that," one guest muttered.

"Maybe," another said, "it was the CIA."

"Nonsense." Vautour quieted such talk with a gruff command. "Our people have *subtlety*."

As he said it, he shifted in his seat, trying to ignore the ache creeping up his bones. His back was killing him. Vautour's lavish dining set, imported from Milan, had started to fall apart apparently. The chair must have had some piece jutting out that stabbed him right in the spine. Vautour resolved to order his assistants to purchase new chairs the very next morning.

***

After dinner, Vautour's guests drifted off, pausing at the door to give Vautour air-kisses and promise to invite him to their own dinner parties. (The prospect annoyed him. One of his friends was into big cats, though lion tasted like shit in Vautour's opinion; another was far too interested in herbal hallucinogens pirated from the Amazon).

When they were gone, Vautour killed time until the midnight hour by drinking several tumblers of 25-year-old scotch in his den, a room full of avian specimens that hadn't made it to the table: herons and spoonbills and nightjars and owlets; birds that died or went rotten before reaching the kitchen. Unwilling to lose an investment, he'd had them all stuffed. His staff spent hours dusting the glorious taxidermy every week. Despite their beauty, and the occasional lick Vautour gave them, the ache in his bones didn't let up.

He was somewhat concerned that the raw kakapo had given him flu-like symptoms, as his body hurt with a dull, pervasive misery difficult to isolate. Vautour, unrepentant, decided to sit for a while in the sauna. That would do the trick: sweat out the pollution. If that didn't work, he could have his personal nurse practitioner come in and pump his stomach. It was a necessary step now and then, such as the time he had that crane torisashi in Kyoto. His nurse practitioner said he almost died; he had merely replied, *hah!*

After ordering his overnight staff out of bed to prepare the sauna,

Vautour made his way to the spa, limping up steps to the east-wing master bedroom *en suite* and pissing aggressively into the toilet. The bidet had barely gotten the chance to finish before he threw off his clothes. Naked, he lumbered to the shower, paying little attention to his broad, meaty body in the wraparound bathroom mirrors. He ran the hot at maximum force and stood under it for several minutes before he saw rivulets of blood running down his ankles. Streams of thin red on the white marble floor. The ache hit him suddenly; sharp, excruciating. He could tell now it emanated from his tailbone. Every time the scalding water touched that spot, Vautour yelped.

He limped over to the intercom to alert his staff something was wrong, but before he reached it he stumbled in front of the sinks. He turned to check his back in the mirror, but his middle was too thick, his spine too inflexible, his ass too broad from years of sitting and boozing and eating rich foods. It felt like someone was stabbing him, but he couldn't see a damned thing. Nothing except the blood leaking down his haunches.

Grimacing through tears and trying not to howl, Vautour grabbed a shaving mirror, positioning it so he could examine himself in the bathroom mirror behind him and find exactly what was bleeding. (Surely it was just an exploded hemorrhoid, or a cut by that damned dining chair. He resolved to sue the manufacturer.) He wiped the steam off the glass, twisted right and left, lifted the magnified mirror several inches before he found it, the source of his pain.

There was a throbbing red hole in his back the size of his fist, and a cluster of black protrusions shivering within it. (How could he have missed such a wound? He was struck dumb with embarrassment. Had he bled on the chair? Left dribbles of blood on his guests' shoes? In an uncharacteristic moment of self-awareness, he wondered if something had been said, something he hadn't paid attention to, that might have warned him this would happen.) The black protrusions moved in and out, dipping, squirming; he watched them for several seconds, the horror outweighing his pain as he squinted. Then he realized what they were.

The feathers of the small stowaway bird were darker now, soaked by his bodily fluids. His blood was sludgy, like tree sap; coagulated. The bird's feet clamped onto the edge of Vautour's wound as though his swollen flesh was the lip of a knothole. The bird dipped into the gore and peeked back out, mimicking a woodpecker that slurped termites and grubs from a chasm in a tree. Behind the bird, Vautour could see a hint of his spine, vertebrae glistening.

As if aware it was being watched, the bird peeked out and went still. Gummy red meat dangled from its beak. It cocked its head as if listening for a far off predator. Such a predator never came; so, as Vautour stood quaking in his shock, it returned to its fleshy burrow.

By the time help arrived, Vautour was on the floor, bleeding out, arms twisted as he grasped at the wound. The EMTs, struggling to identify a weapon, any nearby object that could have demolished the man's spine in such a way, were at a loss. The authorities would have to come in later to determine the source of the attack. (Although one technician, wrestling with the QuickClot gauze, glimpsed a black feather behind the toilet, something she kept to herself. She'd seen the endangered stuffed birds in the den and thought, *what an asshole*.) When they shouted at Vautour to tell them what happened, all they got from him were screams: *it's inside me, it's inside me, it's inside me.*

When I was seven or eight, my mom--
knowing that I enjoyed a good monster cartoon or comic--
picked up a movie for us to watch at Blockbuster.
It was *Alien*.
The chestburster scene
threw me into a panic. I refused to keep watching.

...That being said, I woke up the next morning
and begged to finish it.

Besides high school art and a couple random classes
I took as a child, I have no formal training.
I dropped out of art school because I was more concerned
with watching movies, smoking weed and playing guitar.

If there's one thing I love as
much as making my own art,
it's helping other people make theirs.
Collaboration with like-minded people
is so damn gratifying to me.

Michael Falotico

WILKS ROT

WILKSROT

by Michael Falotico

CDC Blames Rotten Paint/Mold
I'M NOT JUST A MODEL.
I'M A MOVEMENT ARTIST.
THESE PHOTOS OF MY PERFORMANCE AT THE OPENING ARE A COLLABORATION WITH FESTUS!
...BUT, MY SK... IS MY LIVELIHO...
THIS RASH TURNE... LESS THAN A W... AFTER THE OPE...
Shay Gallery Nov 4 1975
CDC Director David Sencer
November 24, 1975
DURING PRODUCTION OF COLDPRESS LINSEED OIL, A MUCILAGE, EMBODIED IN THE OIL, MUST BE REMOVED THROUGH A SERIES OF INDUSTRIAL FILTRATION PROCESSES OR BLACK MOLD WILL OCCUR.
OUR CURRENT HYPOTHESIS IS THAT FESTUS WILKS MUST HAVE BEEN IMPROPERLY MIXING HIS OWN PAINT.
"I SPENT FIFTEEN GRAND ON ONE OF THOSE PIECES OF SHIT."
Doctors Say "STAY HOME"
"LOOK AT ME..."
"THE NEXT TIME LARRY SHAY SHOWS HIS FACE IN NEW YORK, I'M BEATING HIS SCRAWNY ASS INTO THE GROUND!"
Shay Galle... Nov 4 197...
NY ATTORNEY FILES CL... ACTIO... LAWSUIT

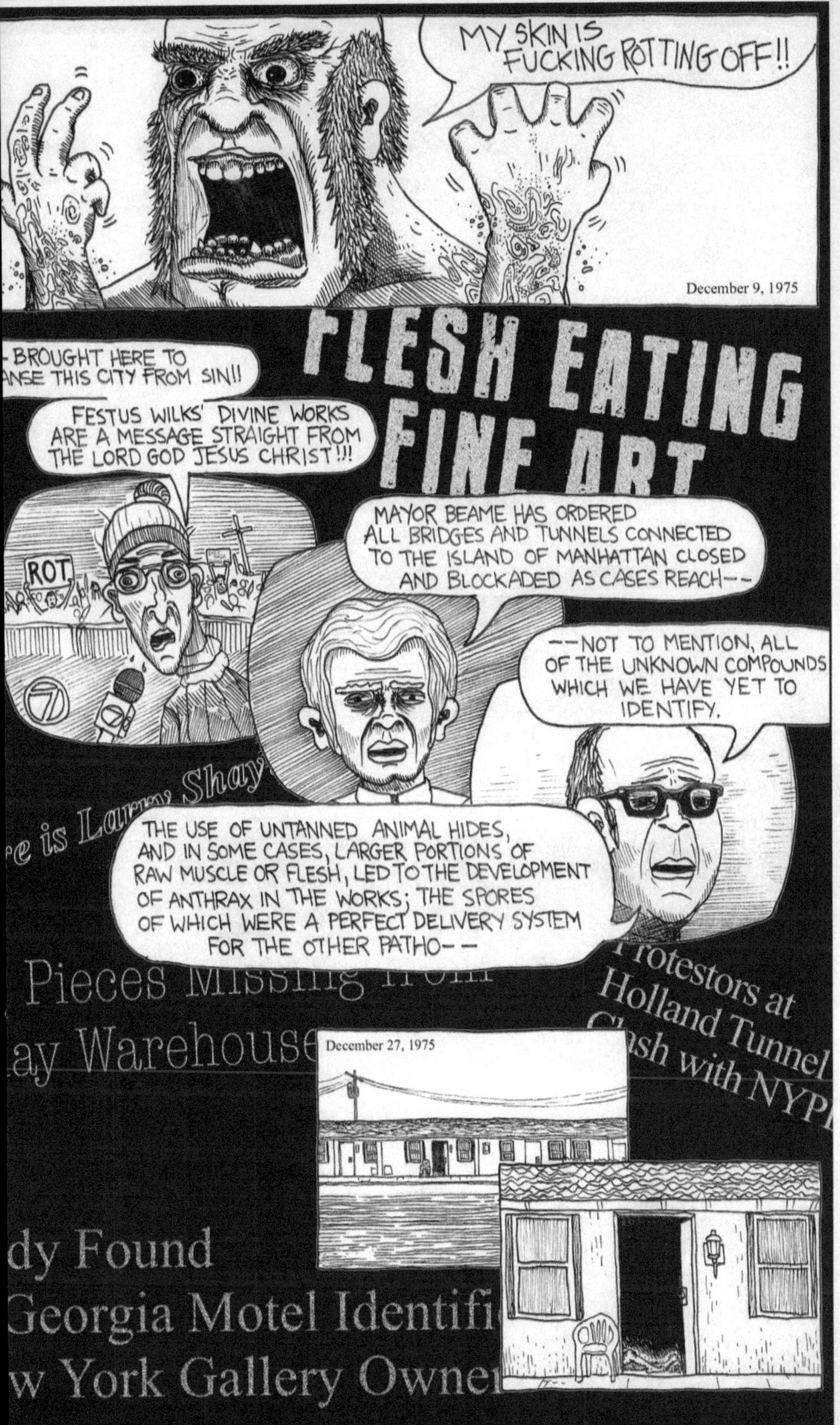
MY SKIN IS FUCKING ROTTING OFF!!

December 9, 1975

FLESH EATING FINE ART

-BROUGHT HERE TO
-ANSE THIS CITY FROM SIN!!

FESTUS WILKS' DIVINE WORKS ARE A MESSAGE STRAIGHT FROM THE LORD GOD JESUS CHRIST!!!

ROT

MAYOR BEAME HAS ORDERED ALL BRIDGES AND TUNNELS CONNECTED TO THE ISLAND OF MANHATTAN CLOSED AND BLOCKADED AS CASES REACH--

--NOT TO MENTION, ALL OF THE UNKNOWN COMPOUNDS WHICH WE HAVE YET TO IDENTIFY.

e is Larry Shay

THE USE OF UNTANNED ANIMAL HIDES, AND IN SOME CASES, LARGER PORTIONS OF RAW MUSCLE OR FLESH, LED TO THE DEVELOPMENT OF ANTHRAX IN THE WORKS; THE SPORES OF WHICH WERE A PERFECT DELIVERY SYSTEM FOR THE OTHER PATHO--

Pieces Missing from

ay Warehouse

Protestors at
Holland Tunnel
Clash with NYP

December 27, 1975

dy Found

Georgia Motel Identifi

w York Gallery Owner

WE NOW BELIEVE THAT THESE COMPOUN
WERE FESTUS WILKS' ATTEMPTS AT MAKIN
HOMEMADE INSECTICIDES AND PLANT GROWTH FORM
DECADES OF REPETITION FORMED A BIOLOGICAL LANDMINE.
WILKS WAS MOST LIKELY USING HIS GARDEN SPRAYERS FOR BOTH HIS YARD WORK AND HIS ART.
PERHAPS THE TWO ARE ONE IN THE SAME?
-- LEFT NO CLUES AS TO HOW THE PIECES WERE SHIPPED TO THE CITY.
WITH THE EXTINCTION OF NEW YORK'S FINE ART COMMUNITY, THE QUESTION ON EVERYONE'S MIND REMAINS: WHO IS FESTUS WILKS?!
STUS W
MAD GENI
THE BIG APPLE ROT
January 22, 1976
CAN YOU GET A CLOSE-UP OF THIS?
IS THAT POSSIBLE?
FOUND ON AN UNDEVELOPED ROLL OF FILM RETRIEVED FROM LARRY SHAY'S APARTMENT, WE NOW HAVE OUR FIRST IMAGE OF WHO WE BELIEVE TO BE OUR PRIME SUSPECT.
Death To
Surpasses
WE ARE NOW WORKING IN COORDINATION W
THE F.B.I. AN
LOCAL PO
IN NEBRA
Remaining Wilks
Pieces Burned in
Undisclosed Location
Cases Found in Staten Island, Broo
Jersey City, Hudson Valley

IF YOU HAVE ANY INFORMATION ABOUT THIS MAN OR THIS ROAD... ✳AACK✳
✳COUGH! COUGH! @ACK!--A'HMM!✳ ✳ EXCUSE ME...
PLEASE CALL THE NUMBER AT THE BOTTOM OF YOUR SCREEN.
MICHAEL FALOTICO 20 21

I was in a secluded spot by the Cimarron River
once... littered along the banks were rusted washers,
discarded furniture, various trash... It made me wonder
how much longer we as a species deserved to last...

...Man treats the planet like an endless buffet.
The fact that we are still allowed to barrel
blindly through is astonishing to me...

Eric Neher

SOMETHING IN THE WHEAT

...It occurred to me...
WHAT IF SOMETHING ELSE
WAS WATCHING US, AND DECIDED
IT COULD DO BETTER?

SOMETHING IN THE WHEAT
BY ERIC NEHER

John Livingston's savior came from above. It streaked through the low hanging gray, burst through the atmosphere and sizzled through the roof of his barn. He watched in disbelief as the flaming projectile bounced off his unkempt yard and shuttled into the middle of his flooded wheat field. He took in all of this while sitting on the front porch of his paint-depleted farmhouse, a cold Bud Light in one hand, a Camel burning in the other.

For a moment, he thought all the smoking and drinking had finally caught up to him and that what he was seeing was the result of a stroke; not an altogether unpleasant prospect. He was drowning, and there was no point in trying to fool himself. The last few years had been hard; even harder since Irene had died.

Something in the Wheat

He gazed over at the empty chair that sat just beyond the wicker table and felt a familiar wave of loneliness wash over him. How long had it been? Three years now? For John, the days on the calendar streamed together like one endless night. It was bad enough having to struggle alone, but next to impossible when Mother Nature seemed to be waging a personal war against him.

"Well," he mumbled, tossing the butt to the ground, "I guess I better check that out."

It was as if a bullet the size of a football had passed through the neglected structure: a clean entry wound near the ridge and a jagged exit wound midway down the eastern wall. A flattened section of switchgrass lay ten feet away from where the projectile had skipped. John made his way to where the soggy stems of next year's mortgage payments drooped like soldiers that had seen enough. There would, of course, be no mortgage payments made with this crop; for there was no crop. What little could be salvaged would be swallowed by the sanctions that had been placed on his biggest buyer.

We'll survive, Irene would have said, grasping his hand while her blue eyes shone with contagious hope. How he longed for those sapphire gems and the comfort they had provided; but she was now nothing more than a phantom. Much like his dream for the future.

The field looked like the Everglades; diseased, mosquito-filled, swamping the plants. John's feet sank into the muck as he pushed into the ruined crop. The once pristine rows were now congested rivers soaking up the late afternoon sun. He sighed and plunged deeper into the waste, cursing to himself.

He tripped over a pair of broken stems and stumbled, then gasped.

Small tendrils of avocado-colored smoke wound their way up from the muddy water. John inched closer and was forced to cover his nose as wafts of melting sludge mingled with the musty air. He heard something that sounded like an egg frying and stopped.

There was a bowl the size of a car in the center of his field. Around its edge ran an ash-capped pile of muck. It was filled with greenish lava that bubbled and popped like thick soup.

"A damn meteor," he said, rubbing his hand across his head. "Well, Irene, that should just about do it." He turned and went back to the house, where another twelve-pack was cooling in the fridge.

That night he sat on the porch long after the sun had fallen. The beer had taken hold, and even Irene's voice was beginning to slur. The forecast tomorrow called for more rain, and now there was a hole in the roof of the barn. Just another nail in the coffin.

John stood up and felt the world begin to spin. He clutched the armrest of Irene's chair and closed his eyes. After a moment, he was able to stumble his way into the house.

The living room looked like a bachelor pad, with unwashed plates littering a coffee table surrounded by empty beer cans. John staggered to the fireplace, its inner hearth looking like a blackened mouth locked in a silent scream. On its shelf sat a row of pictures; captured moments of joy that now brought only pain. Above them, hanging from a pair of hooks, was his ticket out. It was perched like a beacon, daring him to try.

Tonight, perhaps he would.

***

The eastern sky had gone well beyond its early morning haze by the time John stirred. His back felt as stiff as the wood floor he had eventually fallen onto. His arms were numb from cradling the twelve-gauge shotgun, holding it close as he slumbered through the night. A string of icy barbs rippled through his body as he stood and made his way to the fireplace. He hung the gun back on the hooks.

"Soon," he whispered. "Very soon." A searing wedge drove through his skull; for a moment he was sure he was going to black out. The kitchen was only ten feet away but it might as well have been a mile. John aimed himself toward the doorway and slunk to the sink.

He cupped his hands and slammed cold water onto his face. The window above the sink showed the dull gray horizon outside. He tried not to look, tried not to see yet another storm that would soon be raping the remains of his life.

A flash crossing the sky forced his gaze. It was as if he were hypnotized, his eyes locked on to what had to be a dream. Outside, beyond the puddles and past the barn, sat a lush, unharvested field.

John rubbed his eyes and leaned closer to the glass. The field was still there, its wall rippling with each gust of wind. He plowed through the front screen door, knocking loose one of the hinges, and stumbled down the yard, stopping just where the first row of wheat began.

They were perfect. Each plant stood at least five feet tall, with crowning spikes already formed to the point of harvesting. He shut his eyes for a moment, then opened them again. The field radiated life. The ground beneath the plants had the dark tint of fertile soil: dry, but not too dry. All signs of the washout were gone.

"I need a beer," John mumbled, turning back to the house. A hard thud stopped him in his tracks. He spun around, but all he saw was the wheat swaying. Another thump sent an electric charge racing down his spine; he was sure he wasn't alone.

"Who's there?" he cried.

Nothing answered.

Just your imagination, he told himself. His hands shook, but they did that every morning; at least until the second beer had been downed. That was the problem; he hadn't popped the top of his breakfast yet.

A low moan filtered through the wall of green. John let out a squeal and ran through the muddy yard without looking back, certain he would feel dagger-like claws sinking into his shoulder at any moment. A gust of wind slammed against his back, making him stumble.

The porch was suddenly there, and he clipped one of the planks with his shin as he fell headfirst and slid toward Irene's chair. He lay there for a moment, unable to move, his wheezes drowning out all other sounds.

Eventually he rolled over and gazed back at the shimmering wheat.

Something in the Wheat

It waved at him, its green leaves whispering with the voice of the wind.

***

John decided to spend the rest of the day inside, avoiding any window where the field could be seen.

At least, he tried. The beer, of course, was in the fridge. To get to it, he had to pass the kitchen sink, and the window. The trip there was easy enough; he just turned his head the other way and walked by the window. He opened the refrigerator and bent to grab the twelve-pack from the lower shelf, then heard something hit the window. A layer of sweat appeared on his brow, and he fought the urge to scream.

Just keep your eyes up front. A crash of thunder caused him to drop the twelve-pack.

"Shit!" Something moved out of the corner of his eye, but he refused to look. He grabbed the beer and rushed out of the kitchen.

Only after the fifth beer did he feel a semblance of sanity return, and with it a sense of shame. Irene had been dead three years now. Her cancer-riddled body was buried a mile away in their family plot. What would she say if she saw him now? When she was alive he rarely drank; he had kept his smoking to just five cigarettes a day, and never around her.

Now he had given up, had let the farm go to hell; and yes, the rain had caused damage, but still…he could have done more. The filth surrounding him was proof of that.

"I'm sorry," he said to the growing shadows.

Outside, the cloud-buried sun made its way toward the western horizon. This had been Irene's favorite time; when the day's work came to a close. An image of her sitting in her chair, waiting for him, played out like a favorite rerun. They would meet on the porch each evening like birds returning to roost and share a plate of raisin cookies she had baked the day before; always his favorite.

But this memory always ended the same way, with her face darkening, becoming pale and sunken. The mental portrait of her final days crept its way into his dreams no matter how much he drank. The withered texture of her sunken skin; how she had gripped his hand in her last minute; her panicked blue eyes trying to focus past the morphine fog, wanting only to know that he was there.

And had she seen him? Did she even realize that he was sitting beside her bed, tears flowing down his cheeks? This was the unanswered question that had sent him reeling into whatever bottle he could find. A guilty burden he would never be able to lay down.

A yip ripped through the night, snapping his thoughts back to the darkening room; just a coyote preparing to hunt. John closed his eyes for a moment, listening to the hypnotic pittering of rain on the roof. With a grunt, he stood and went back into the kitchen, stopping at the sink.

He peeked through the glass. The field still stood tall.

***

The rain ended by ten that night; by then, John was numb. He had half a mind to go back out to his field, dark or not, find *whatever* had scared the shit out of him, and shoot it. He staggered over and took the shotgun off the hooks, grabbed his beer, and charged out the front door, making it as far as the edge of the porch before pausing.

There was still the field itself. What had made it healthy overnight? Not just *healthy*: the best crop he had ever seen. Was it connected to whatever was moving around in there?

Suddenly the shadows covering the earth seemed to be much more than just something void of light. It was as if he were surrounded by some kind of ancient sea, and within it circled throwback beasts patiently awaiting their next meal. The thought was enough to steer him away from the edge and back to his chair.

John popped another beer and took a contemplative swig; this fear was something...strange. Losing Irene had been scary, but at least it was rational; people live and people die.

This was different. Never had he felt such terror over something he couldn't explain. It was probably just a deer; at worst a cougar, which was easy enough to handle with the shotgun. So why this irrational fear? Why did the thought of entering the field fill him with dread?

"Because the field ain't natural, that's why," he said to the night air. "*Something* brought that wheat back to life."

John went back inside, shutting and locking the door behind him. He went to the kitchen and closed the curtain, then checked the back door lock. Irrational or not, his fear was real. He decided to go back to the field at first light and face it.

The phone rang. He stared at it from the kitchen doorway. The receiver lit up with each trill. Shortness of breath seized him as he waited for the person on the other end to give up, but it continued to ring.

Finally, John picked up the handset.

"Hello," he said.

"John, it's Barry."

Relief flowed over him. He felt foolish. Barry Jones was his neighbor...if one could be considered a neighbor out in the flooded wastelands. His farm had suffered the same fate as everyone else's along the plains, leaving him with a third mortgage and an absent wife who had finally had enough.

"How are you, Barry?" said John.

"Well, I'm not sure," said Barry.

"What's going on?"

"Look, this is going to sound crazy," Barry said. "My cornfields have come back. I know it's not possible, but they have."

"What are you talking about?" John's grip tightened on the phone.

"The night before last I heard something outside, it sounded like a plane had crashed. I went out and I saw something smoking in my field." He paused for a moment; John could tell he was struggling to keep calm.

"And?" said John.

"There was a big hole right in the middle of the corn. I figured maybe part of a satellite had landed, or a meteor, but it was dark and there was nothing I could do, so I went back to the house. The next morning I went out and there it was."

"Have you told anyone else?" asked John.

"Hell no. I wasn't even sure I should tell you. Have you seen anything strange?"

John considered telling Barry about his field but decided against it. Maybe it was the thought of the news spreading, which could bring all kinds of unwanted people onto his land. Maybe he didn't want to deal with the authorities, especially in his fragile state of mind. The truth, however, was something he didn't want to admit, even to himself: John had become quite comfortable wallowing in his misery.

"Nothing like that has happened here," he said.

"Well, I know it sounds crazy, but you should come over and take a look," said Barry. "The plants are six feet tall and the ears are a foot long."

"I'll try to get by there in the next day or so," said John. "Barry, just be careful."

"Oh, don't worry about me. I've got some ears boiling as we speak."

John put the receiver back in its cradle. Maybe he should have told Barry. What if whatever was going on was dangerous? Barry hadn't mentioned seeing anything *in* his cornfield...but that didn't mean there wasn't.

And what about the moaning in the wheat? What had that been? He'd like to say it was just the wind, but he had heard plenty of gusts racing through his fields and never anything like that.

He left the kitchen and flopped onto the couch. At least Barry had his corn crop back. That's when it hit John; he now had his crop back, too.

And what a crop it was! Even with the sanctions, he was sure to come out ahead. The loans would be paid off; all that would be left was his mortgage. John leaned back and let his mind wander. If he could get one more crop like this next year, he could sell this shithole and get the hell out of Dodge. An image of blue water splashing over his toes led him gently to sleep.

***

John's eyes flew open; his breath came in gasps. The room was dark, the only light the silver beams of a waning moon filtering through the window behind the couch.

A crash rocked the front door. John's heart leapt and he reached for the shotgun. He pointed the gun at the door, but there was only silence. He shivered in the shadows long enough for the gun to become heavy in his hands. Finally, he stood up and made his way to the door. He disengaged the lock and turned the knob.

There was nothing there. John gazed into the pitch, out to where the wall of wheat sat hidden within the darkness. He tilted his head, trying to listen, but all he heard was the continued whispering of the shrouded crop.

Something on the porch rattled. John flicked his lighter and held it out. There, just on the other side of the door, was a shadow darker than the night.

It flopped around like a thing on fire. He walked over and saw that it was a crow. One of its wings was bent awkwardly; its head lolled like it was on a swivel. It wasn't hard to figure out what had happened. It had obviously flown into the door…but *why*?

Crows don't come out at night.

John knelt for a closer look. The bird came toward him, stopping next to his foot; John saw glistening streams leaking out of its beak. Suddenly it let out a squawk and snapped at his boot. John shot up and stepped back. The bird pushed its broken body closer, coming to a stop at his foot, and continued to peck away at the leather boot.

John watched with shocked fascination. With little else to do, he lifted his foot and brought it down on the bird's skull. He kicked the body off the porch and went back into the house.

He grabbed a beer out of the fridge and went to the couch. Perhaps it had some kind of disease, some new avian flu that he hadn't heard of yet. Or maybe it was nothing more than a bird that had knocked itself crazy.

John decided to take a closer look when the sun came up.

***

It was well after ten before he finally stumbled to the bathroom to relieve his bladder. The late morning air felt wet as he walked out onto the porch. He felt sweat already beginning to form. At least it didn't look like it was going to rain.

The crow lay where he had kicked it. John stepped off the porch and knelt beside the bird. There didn't seem to be anything out of the ordinary, no foaming at the mouth or dried mucus around the eyes. It was just dead.

The field stood as green as the day before. There should have been relief in knowing that he had been saved from utter ruin, but he couldn't shake the feeling that had been gnawing at him since it first appeared.

Maybe I should call Barry and make sure everything is alright.

John was headed back into the house when something moved within the first row of wheat. A chill seized him as he realized he had left the shotgun leaning against the couch.

A raccoon stepped out of the wheat into the yard, coming to a stop a few feet away from the field. John felt his heart slow and realized he had been holding his breath. The raccoon looked at him, its small hands kneading the grass. John released a long sigh and turned back to the house when a sudden brown blur burst through the green wall.

The raccoon screamed as the antlers of an eight-point buck pierced its body. The buck rose and brought its spears back down. The raccoon lay skewered, its small body writhing. The buck pushed until John heard the raccoon's cracking ribs; then it became still.

John leapt onto the porch. The deer raised its head, the bloody body hanging from its antlers. Its eyes locked on John; for a moment John was sure they had flashed emerald green.

Something in the Wheat

The deer dashed straight for him. John reached the door and dove headfirst through the opening, kicking it shut just as the buck rammed its head into the stained oak. The tips of two antlers burst through, their bloodsoaked points inches from where John's feet braced the panel.

The wood splintered as the deer struggled to free itself. John turned the deadbolt, then rolled to where the shotgun was leaning against the couch. An ear-splitting screech caused him to cringe as the buck tore its antlers free. John jumped to his feet, pumping a shell into the chamber of the gun, and pointed it at the door. He heard the animal's hooves clicking on the porch; he considered trying to get a shot from the window, but his legs refused to work.

There was a scream in the distance, followed by a heavy thud. Then all was quiet. John stood with the gun still aimed at the door, sweat pouring down his face. Finally, he felt the adrenaline subside. He lowered the gun and made his way to the window, pushing the curtain aside.

Nothing moved. The porch was empty. Just beyond the steps, he could see the ripped body of the raccoon laying in the grass. *Murdered and mutilated by a deer. Why would a deer do that?* He had heard of them attacking people in self defense. But to kill a raccoon? And not just kill it, but massacre it, like it had some kind of vendetta...

After double-checking the front door lock, John went to the kitchen. He looked through the window.

The image was Norman Rockwell perfect. Blue skies hung over his brilliant, money-making crop.

It had to be the wheat.

He thought of Barry. A rush of anger went through him for not saying anything the night before. But Barry didn't have wheat, he had corn. *Would that make a difference?* John doubted it.

Then a thought broke through that turned his throat desert dry: Barry had been boiling up that corn to eat it.

***

The phone trilled away as John gazed out the kitchen window, his mind racing. The field stared back at him. He was sure he could hear it. Was it calling to him?

Of course, that had to be his imagination, yet there was something welcoming about those blades gently waving.

The line on the other end stopped ringing, and for a moment John thought that it had been disconnected. He was about to hang up when a sound like someone trying to breathe in a plastic bag came over the line.

"Barry?" said John. "Are you there?" The rasping became louder, sounding like an obscene phone call.

"Barry, is that you?"

"John, I don't feel so well."

"Hang on," said John. "I'm coming over."

John hung up and grabbed his keys and his shotgun. He considered grabbing a beer too, but decided against it. His old Ford truck was sitting under the carport on the other side of the house. He made his way to it, eyeing the field as he did. Nothing moved; there was no sound except the whisper.

The truck bounced down the quarter-mile gravel driveway. On each side was a rippling sea of green, going well beyond his property for as far as the eye could see. A pair of coyotes rushed out of the field to his right; he slammed the brakes. They fled into the wheat on the other side.

Following close behind was a small herd of deer, their hides matted and ripped. John could see one of the deer's exposed ribs, blood pouring from the wound. They continued after the coyotes, plunging into the field without noticing him.

John sat for a moment, his heart hammering in his chest. It was as if the world had turned upside down. The prey had become predator, the predator prey. Was this because of the crops?

How could it not be?

I have some ears boiling as we speak. John groaned and continued down the driveway.

Barry's house was five miles away. He gripped the steering wheel until his knuckles were about to come through the skin. A river of fear flooded over him. Why hadn't he just told Barry the truth?

On each side of the road stood ominous foliage, green and fertile. Surely this couldn't be just a local event. Someone had to know something. Barry turned on the radio and was greeted by static. He turned the dial until he found something trying to come through.

It was from a station out of Tulsa.

There seems to be a rash of animal attacks, the woman said.

"No shit," said John, gazing from left to right.

The best thing to do is stay out of the country until Wildlife and Game can sort it out.

And that was it. Nothing about the strange crops that had sprung up overnight. Nothing about the meteors. Just *stay out of the country.*

Barry's driveway was on the left. John slowed and turned in. The house sat a hundred yards back; John could see Barry's Dodge sitting beside the garage. He then saw something that made his heart sink. It was a cherry red Lincoln. It belonged to Barry's estranged wife.

***

The front door was wide open. John stood for a moment, shotgun in hand. No noise came from inside the house. It seemed as if the entire world had fallen into deathly silence. The only sound was the occasional breeze blowing through the cornfield that surrounded Barry's house like sentinels. John stepped to the door and was immediately hit by a smell that made him gag. He covered his mouth and moved back.

"Barry," he coughed out. "Are you in there?" No answer.

He was suddenly sure that coming here had been a bad idea. There was no rational reason to think that, but he had given up on being rational the moment a rabid deer had tried to kill him.

"Okay," he said, backing off the porch. "I'm going to head home, but I'll call you later."

He was turning toward his truck when something dark flew out of the doorway and landed at his feet. John looked down and felt his stomach flip. A scream tried to escape from his throat but was blocked by an urge to vomit. Weakness shot down his legs; he tripped over his own feet and fell to the ground, landing inches away from where the head of Barry's wife now sat. Her glazed eyes were locked on his own in frozen terror.

"Holy shit!"

"We're going to be fine," said a resonant voice.

John looked up. There at the doorway was Barry. He was completely naked, his skin covered in crimson as if he had been dipped in red paint. His hand was on a long butcher knife.

"Barry, what have you done?"

Barry stepped out of the doorway and into the sunlight, his eyes reflecting emerald green.

"It's time for us to harvest, John," said Barry. "It's time for us to share our gift with the world."

John stood and stepped back, gripping the shotgun. "What are you talking about?"

"We are the ones chosen for the cleansing," said Barry. "The ones who must clear the way."

"Why did you kill your wife?"

"Because I had to prove myself and because she was a bitch. Mostly because she was a bitch."

"Prove yourself to who?"

Barry smiled conspiratorially.

"They're coming, John. As soon as the fruits of our labor reach the masses they'll come, and as long as we help them we'll be okay."

"Who is coming?"

"The ones who saved us. The ones who gave us back our fields. They were looking for a new home and they have found it."

"So the animals...our crops made them act like that?"

"Look at them as test subjects," said Barry. "What you're seeing is just the beginning."

"They're going to kill everything?" said John.

"Not at all. They're going to wait while we kill ourselves."

"I can't be a part of this."

"You have no choice."

"Really?" said John. "I'm going back to my truck and if you try coming at me with that knife I'll blow you in half."

"I will not try to hurt you, John. You are one of the chosen, but I will tell you this: my cornfields have spread. Some as far as Wileys Creek to the west and some as far as your family cemetery to the east. Do you know what that means, John?"

"I don't care," said John, backing away towards his truck. Barry stood with the knife hanging at his side. John fumbled for the handle of the door, never taking his eyes off Barry.

He slid into the truck and started the motor, placing the shotgun across his lap. Barry seemed to have lost interest and made his way to where his wife's head now sat. A cloud of flies swarmed around her blood-soaked hair. John put the truck into reverse just as Barry drove the knife through her skull, lifting it until his face was even with hers.

He turned it towards John and said, "Until death do we part." Then he went back inside, slamming the door behind him.

***

The road back was littered with animals, but John didn't seem to notice. He was trying to keep the contents of his stomach down and the image of Barry's wife out of his mind. It didn't work; he pulled over and opened the door. The shakes had returned and it took three attempts to wipe his mouth. A sudden pain struck his chest, sending bolts down both arms; for a moment he was sure he was having a heart attack.

Clearing the way so they could come, Barry had said. Who? The government? John sat back in the seat and closed his eyes, listening to the hammering of his heart. Finally, he was able to pull the truck back out onto the road and drive the last couple of miles home.

***

That evening found him again with a beer in his hand, seated on the porch with his shotgun close. The yard was filled with opossums, raccoons and skunks scattered throughout the grass like a C.S. Lewis battleground. The sun was sinking past the endless growing horizon and still, he hadn't called anyone about Barry.

He knew that he should, and that other lives could very well be at risk. What if Barry decided to go into town? What if he decided to pay a visit to the local grocery store? Would he be dressed? Would he be going up and down the aisles with the head of his wife stuck on a knife? John shuddered, but couldn't make the call.

The wheat whispered even though there was barely a breeze. John tried to ignore it, but it seemed as though he could hear words trying to form.

The sun touched the top of the green wall, casting shadows close to where he sat; they slithered forward like a nest of awoken snakes. The thought of those shadows reaching him was terrifying, like a shroud meant to smother his soul. John finished his beer, grabbed his gun, and went inside.

***

John slept on the couch, his arm draped over the shotgun barrel. Nothing slammed against the door that night. There was no creaking porch or ghostly moaning.

But there were still dreams; Barry, holding his wife's head as he lumbered naked into his cornfield; a herd of skinless deer racing over the countryside, their bloodsoaked antlers decorated with the ripped hides of their victims. These dreams flickered in and out like an old movie reel until finally coming to a stop at the edge of his wheat field.

"I'll see you soon," something whispered.

John sat up; his chest shot fireworks down his arms as he fought for air. Outside was pale blue, the sun just peeking up from the east. John rose and opened the front door. The yard was calm…empty. He clutched the door frame. It *was* empty; all the dead animals were gone.

He quickly shut and locked the door, then went to the fridge and saw that he had an even bigger problem. He was down to his last twelve-pack. Could he dare a trip to town? It would mean having to drive by Barry's again.

No, not yet. He could make this last a day. He popped the top off the first one and walked back to the couch, turning on the T.V. Maybe there would be news about Barry and he wouldn't have to worry, but none of the stations were coming through.

"Not good," he said, switching off the tube. He took a quick pull from the can and went to the kitchen window. The field was now over eight feet tall, its leaves looking like double-edged swords. Perhaps he should go ahead and risk the trip and buy as much beer as the fridge could hold. It would probably be his last chance, and if the end was nigh he preferred to face it drunk off his ass. He was just turning from the window when something caught his eye, forcing him to forget everything else.

"This can't be," he said. "Please don't do this to me." He stumbled his way to the living room, grabbing the shotgun. The front door was locked; for a moment the deadbolt refused to turn.

"C'mon, you bastard…" Finally the door opened. John stepped onto the front porch and froze. A plate with neatly stacked cookies had been placed on the wicker table. Ripened raisins poked through the baked dough just like he remembered, sprinkled with small seeds, their greenish hue reflecting in the sunlight.

"This can't be," he said again, dropping the gun and falling to his knees.

"But it is," the wheat whispered. "Our gift to you."

John looked toward the field just as Irene stepped out of its lush edge. Her hair flamed red in the early morning light; her face was alive, radiant, beautiful. She wore the same flowered dress he had bought for her funeral, and it still looked as new as the day he had closed the casket.

"How...?" he said.

"It is their gift to you, their gift to us," said Irene as she walked toward the porch. "It is what they offer in return for our help."

"Who are they?" he said.

"They are the new owners, and they've come to clean up our mess."

"I don't understand."

"Of course you don't." Irene ascended the steps. "But you will." She passed by him, looking not a day over twenty-five. John felt desire flood over him, a feeling he had almost forgotten.

"I've missed you so much."

"I know you have," she said, sitting down in her chair. She reached over and patted his chair. "Here, come sit beside me."

It was then that he noticed her eyes. The blue was gone, switched to green, as green as Barry's had been as he had held his wife's severed head. John walked to the chair and stopped.

"Don't be afraid of me," she said. "Please don't be scared."

John looked down at his wife. Her face displayed the same sadness that had always been able to mellow him, no matter how angry he might have been, extinguishing any thoughts of running. And why would he? He was dying anyway; killing himself because of the open wound that losing her had left. If this was to be the end, then so be it. At least her face would be the last thing that he would ever see. John sank into his chair.

"What do I have to do?" he said.

Irene reached over and placed her hand on his leg. It felt warm and alive.

"Just have a cookie and the answers will come."

John reached for the plate and took one, and together they watched as the sun continued to rise.

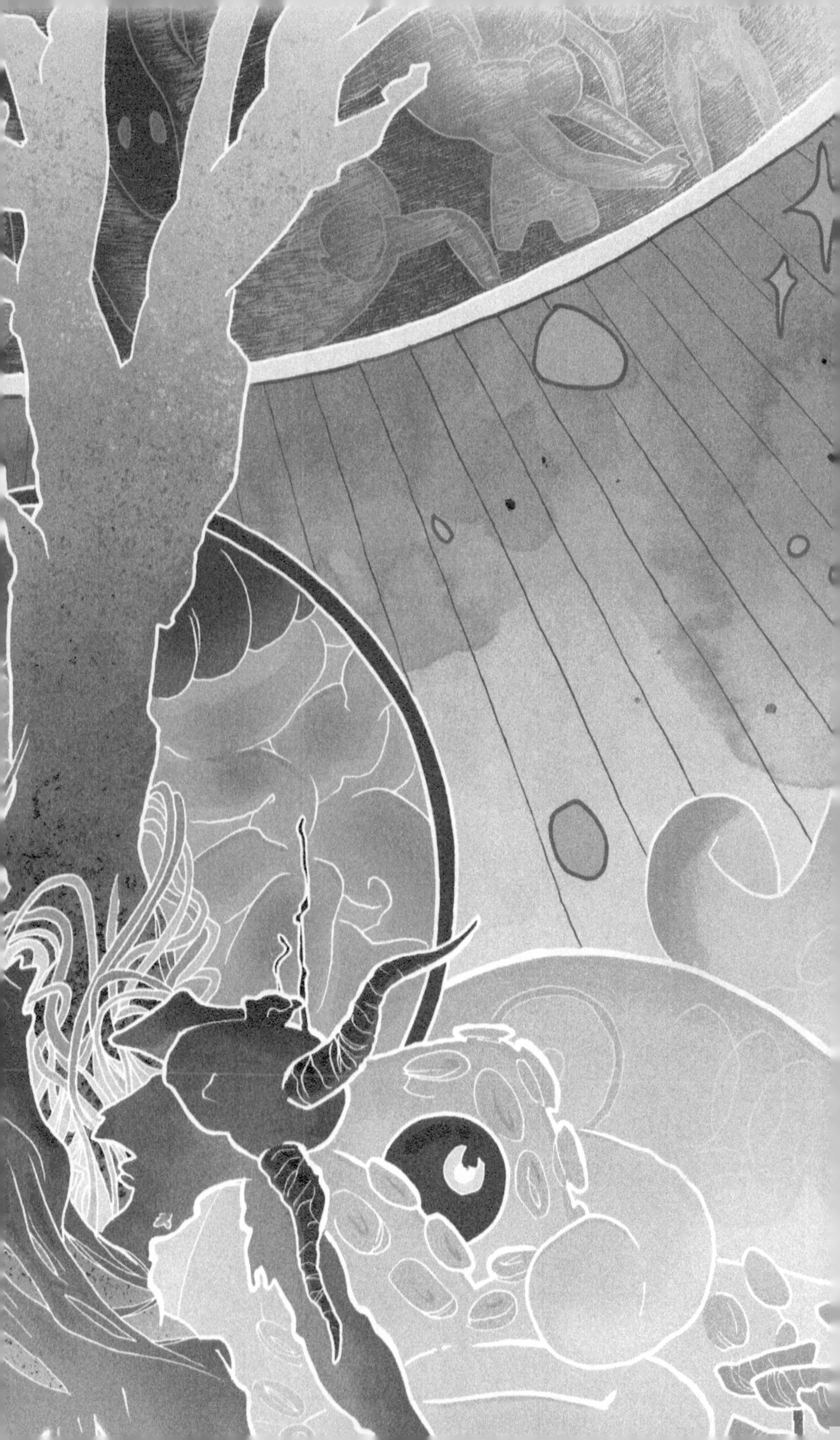

Green Inferno

SNIIIIIF
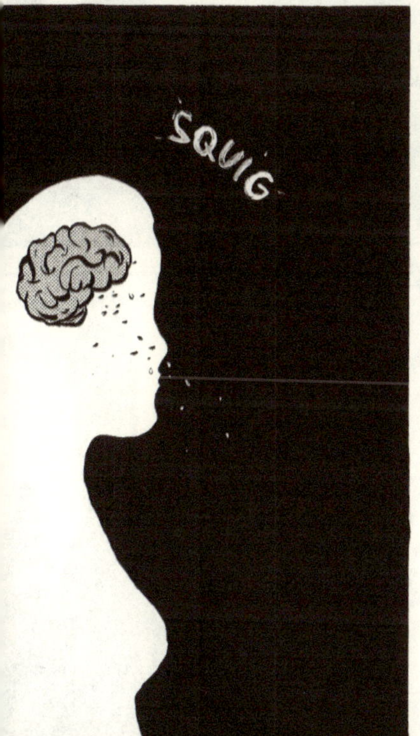
SQUIG

SQUIGGLE

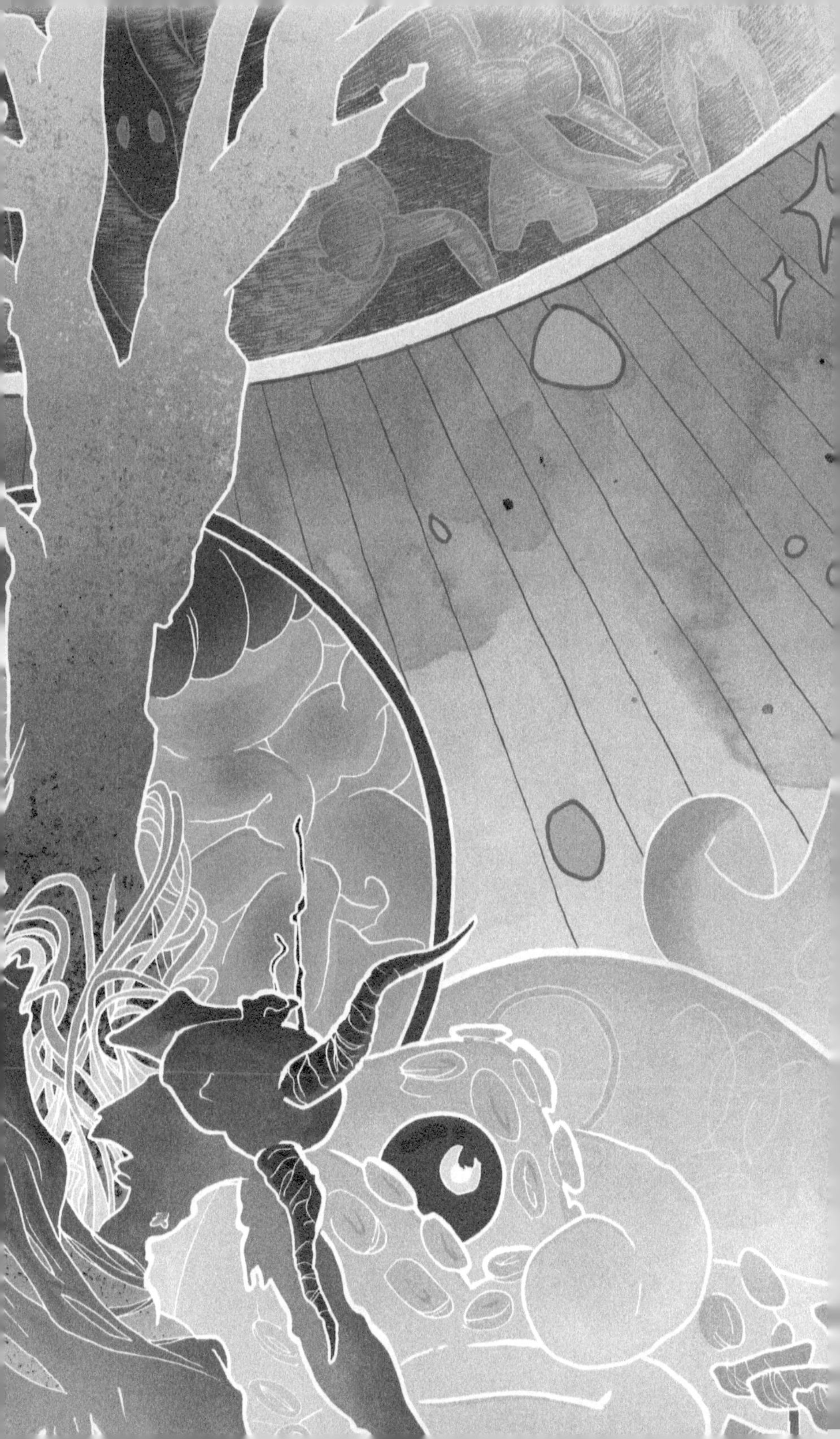

My father once told me the story of a
cursed rice cooker...The unexplainable can be
attributed to kami, or spirits. He would say,
"KAMI WILL CURSE YOU IF YOU NEGLECT THEM."

He [was referring to] TSUKUMOGAMI: tools
that have become self-aware due to their
longevity... If you can't take good care of
[your tools], you'd best not worship them.

Umiyuri Katsuyama

translated by Toshiya Kamei

THE GUARDIAN ON NEW YEAR'S EVE

As the old saying goes:
THE SPIRIT YOU DO NOT APPROACH
WON'T HURT YOU.

THE GUARDIAN ON NEW YEAR'S EVE
BY UMIYURI KATSUYAMA
TRANSLATED BY TOSHIYA KAMEI

As the year nears its end, my mother and I busy ourselves with preparations for the New Year. That said, we don't go out of our way. Instead of cooking from scratch, we order ready-made osechi and have it delivered from a department store. We tidy up around the house, put up shogatsu decorations, and cook black beans over a slow fire. That's about it.

Also, as the old year gives way to the new, demons and ghosts attempt to sneak in, so we hang a scroll depicting the deity Zhong Kui to protect our home. Dressed in an ancient Chinese clerical robe, the bushy-browed, thick-bearded demon hunter glares at the viewer with his ring-shaped eyes. He would surely scare any evil spirit away. My father cleans the living room window with crumpled newspaper. He polishes the glass until it becomes practically transparent. Then he ties up a stack of old newspapers and puts it away in the shed.

A few days ago, my brother, who lives by himself in a distant city, phoned me to tell me he's too busy to come home this year.

"Hey, Kazuma. Don't forget to put up the Zhong Kui scroll Mom gave you," I reminded him. "The one she handed to you when you moved out, okay? You think we're superstitious, but I'm serious. I mean it."

"Yeah, yeah, yeah. Okay, little sis," he said, sounding unconvinced and noncommittal. I could picture his wry sneer curving his lips on the other end of the line.

"I don't have it," he mumbled at last.

"What do you mean? Don't tell me you lost it!"

"I sold it. I had no choice. Don't tell Mom, okay? I don't want her to worry."

I remained silent.

"Gotta go. Love ya. Bye." Then he hung up.

In the evening, my folks and I stand in front of the kamidana with clasped hands to welcome the arrival of Toshigami-sama, the deity of the new year. Then we bow heads and say brief prayers wishing for a peaceful end of the year. Afterward, we sit around the kotatsu and poke the sukiyaki pot with chopsticks for tidbits. Shrimps, tuna sashimi, sunomono salad, and gratin—my brother's favorite dish—fill the table. But an empty spot at the kotatsu reminds me of his absence, and it practically ruins my appetite. *The Red and White Singing Contest* on NHK fails to cheer me up.

"Sumire!" Mother cries, startling me. Like me, she's got a keen sixth sense, but hers is even keener. She seems to have sensed something is amiss with my brother. "Draw Zhong Kui for Kazuma!"

"Can I just take a photo of our Zhong Kui?"

"No, that won't do. He's busy watching over our home now."

I grab a sketchbook and a brush pen and make my best attempt to draw the Chinese demon hunter. Father would usually complain about interrupting our meal, worrying about the meat getting overcooked. But even he turns serious, sensing emergency in my mother's voice.

With each brushstroke, a misshapen, pot-bellied figure takes shape. I add round eyes, an unruly mop of hair, and a bushy beard. I glance toward my mother, and she nods, urging me to continue. I'm horrible at drawing, but I've got to keep going, to defeat something. Something? I don't know what it is . . . I just feel it in my bones. Some sinister force crawls toward my brother.

"Looks great, hon." Mother gently places her hand on my shoulder. "Send it to your brother *now*."

With a trembling hand, I snap a photo of my drawing with my phone and shoot it his way.

"C'mon, Kazuma! Open it, please!" I mumble under my breath as I stare at the screen, waiting for the message to say "read." Waiting for a response. But as the clock strikes midnight, the message only reads "delivered."

INVERSUS II.
IN THE SEA, THE STARS
"It's like a dream," Vi offered, heart in her throat. Agent Akeley knew better than to christen it with such a honeyed name; this was a nightmare.

...Would you believe I didn't even think of this
as a murder mystery while I was writing it?
That said, I am a pretty big mystery fan--classic
Poirot and Holmes, along with newer ones--
so I certainly had those influences to guide me...

There's a huge volume of Horror fiction
about white, straight, able-bodied cishet
people...there are more stories you can tell
if you step out of that model...Diversity
of character makes for more engaging stories...

...I thought about how much responsibility
is placed on childcare workers, and how
scary it would be to be suddenly saddled
with life-or-death responsibilities in a
position of marginal authority.

Spencer Koelle

THE SPARE CHILD

Humans are good at killing off
things that hunt humans...
WE'VE GOTTEN USED TO THE IDEA THAT
WE EXIST OUTSIDE THE FOOD WEB.

THE SPARE CHILD
BY SPENCER KOELLE

Violent rain blurred the shore, sea and air together. Kendra was soaked before she made it from the dock to the parking lot. She caught her cane on an invisible groove, then yelped as she went face first into the railing.

The light from the Jersey Bay Museum slipped through the wooden slats. It glinted on slime and water. A coin fell from Kendra's pocket into the bay. Something purple and red flexed away from it, maybe a cuttlefish or a freshly molted lobster. Lightning struck. By the time Kendra regained her night sight, there was nothing to be seen. She straightened up and hobbled down the concrete ramp.

She didn't know what had happened with the two staff members who were supposed to be watching the edutainment slumber party at Bayside Discovery Project. She'd come in because she really needed the hours, and because the mission was close to her heart. She reminded herself of this as sea spray backhanded her and the fifth car pulled up.

"Welcome to Bayside Slumber Night! We inspire people to take care of the environment, culture and history of New Jersey's Bayside region through preservation, education and example. Does everyone have the follow-up payment of check, voucher or cash?"

A dusting of hail glinted in five sets of narrow headlights and attacked five rusty car roofs. At least there weren't any Boy Scout troops or family groups to deal with; just single children.

"Can you please be taking American Express credit cards?" one of the parents shouted through thick wind and a thicker accent. Another parent shoved a soggy check into her hands. The people were just glints of white teeth and umbrellas in the darkness. Small colorful raincoats swarmed around her, squealing in excitement and distress. Kendra hurried the shrouded children into the building. She watched the window as the children hung up their raincoats. The last flash of taillights vanished. Kendra knew the lights of town were just around the curve in the road, but all she saw was reflected streetlight and snapping shadows.

She turned back to the six shivering children. "Who wants hot chocolate?"

***

Kendra gave up on the new combination hot beverage/espresso machine. She picked up her cane and slammed the kettle on the stove. Earl was supposed to help her with setup.

He must be checking the backup generator or testing the hand-rail structural integrity. The man was obsessed with safety measures.

"Let's start by introducing ourselves, along with our favorite marine animal," Kendra said. She waved at the Touch Tank and the Interactive Wetlands Ecosystem display.

The first child to raise a hand wore outgrown dark clothes, frosted styled hair, and lots of temporary tattoos. Kendra recognized the purple shapeshifter and electric mouse from her nephew's favorite TV show, along with an *ophiotaurus*. The child also had a lightning-cleft skull on the back of one hand; the other hand sported a laughing mouth and a bloodshot eye. Their eyes darted around Kendra without ever settling on her. He/she/they opened their mouth to speak, closed it, and fidgeted with a rainbow bracelet while the silence grew. "The mimic octopus is changey and mysterious," they said haltingly. "I'm Taylor and they can change color like a chameleon and they change shape and texture too!"

"I'm Adriana," said a white girl in trendy overalls with a vaguely European accent. She had light-up sneakers, a plain black fanny pack, and short curly hair. "I can't wait to make the planet a better place and I really like it here. Oh, um, the coolest thing in the ocean is the mantis shrimp." Kendra turned to a girl who was snapping her gum and staring vacantly at the collection of shipwreck artifacts. She looked Kendra in the eye. "My name is Sophie and I have a puppy," she announced.

Kendra waited for the follow-up. Hail pelted against the roof while a high wave whipped the deck outside. Some of the other kids looked at her. Sophie tugged her long brown hair and smiled.

"And what's your favorite *marine* animal?" Kendra prompted. She edged her chair toward the ocean food chain display. "Octopi? Shrimps? Horseshoe crabs maybe?"

Sophie turned her dreamy gaze to the barely-audible looped video above the gift shop counter. "Dolphins are intelligent and graceful," she said. Kendra nodded.

"Electric eels because they can zap people," said a surly boy in a Spider-Man shirt. "My name's Thomas, and I think trains are stupid." He glared around as if daring somebody to contradict him.

"Yes, Thomas," Kendra said in what she hoped was a soothing tone. "Did you know that electric rays have even stronger voltage than the eel, and some of them live near the Jersey Shore?"

Thomas feigned interest in the *USS Meerwyld in High Storm* painting on the other side of the room. It showed brilliant cresting waves, but Kendra suspected his main intent was to show contempt.

"How about you..." she pointed to the boy with a tie dye shirt, yellow shorts and neon green fingernails.

"I'm Sancho," he said, twisting his shirt nervously, "and I like sea slugs because they're weird and colorful and pretty." Adriana raised an eyebrow. Sophie and Taylor smiled at him.

Kendra turned to the sixth camper, a quiet little girl with a nut brown dress. The child fiddled with her embroidered turquoise headscarf and looked down.

"Hello," Kendra said, trying to sound non-threatening. "What's your name?"

"Fareeda," she murmured.

"And what's your favorite sea creature?" Kendra encouraged.

Fareeda collected herself before answering. "I like the megamouth sharks because they're big and friendly and, um, they don't hurt anyone but I think it's amazing that they existed in the ocean for so long but we didn't discover that giant fish until thirty years ago." She retreated into her clothing with a nervous giggle.

"Sharks eat people," Thomas snapped. Fareeda flinched.

"Actually, megamouths are one of three sharks that feed on plankton, the tiny plants and animals that make up the bottom of the ocean food chain," Kendra said. She walked over to Thomas. "Please use your indoor voice."

Thomas's squirm suggested she'd won a tactical advantage. She reminded herself that winning a battle of wills with a small boy wasn't anything to be proud of.

Adriana raised her hand. "We already know about plankton. It's right up there on the wall," she complained.

"I didn't know about plankton," Fareeda said with a mixture of apology and defiance.

"Me neither!" said Sancho, smiling at Kendra.

"Me neither!" Sophie added.

Kendra settled into her chair. "Well, I guess some of you are going to learn a little more tonight, and that's okay. If you really get bored with the material, there's lots of books you can read about the history of the shore and wildlife in your own backyard."

The screaming kettle jolted Kendra upright. A distant lightning flash stretched rusty oystering relics into unreal light and oily shadows.

"Who knows about the Exxon oil spill?" Kendra said, ignoring the jolts of pain as she balanced the heavy tray of hot chocolate mugs with both hands.

Adriana, Fareeda and Thomas raised their hands. Sophie looked around before raising hers. Taylor stared blankly while Sancho squirmed.

"Thomas, could you explain it for the rest of the group?" Kendra said.

Thomas folded his hands behind his back.

"My dad said that these rich guys at Exxon-Mobil were too greedy and the government wasn't doing its job so another offshore oil rig broke again, and there's poison gas leaking into the ocean. Lots of seals and plants and whales are getting hurt and there's gunk all over the shores and the fishing's going to be ruined again." Thomas panted for breath, looking nervous but proud.

"Right," Kendra said. "Ocean pollution is a big problem." She turned back to the desk and glanced at her lesson plan:

At this point, the visitors try a fun experiment to see how fast pollution spreads and the different ways to clean it up.

This required safety goggles, sponges and other supplies from the science lab cabinet.

The wind howled and waves roared while Kendra fumbled with the unyielding lock. She remembered she didn't have the science lab key and bit back a curse. *Time to think fast.*

"I've got some marine life coloring books I'd like you to fill out," she said, pulling the sheets from the art supplies cabinet. Kendra handed them out along with crayon boxes on her way to the elevator. *This should keep them occupied.*

***

The elevator groaned as it crawled upwards. Kendra wondered if anyone ever bothered to check the inspection certificate on file.

"Earl?" she called as soon as the doors opened. "I need the key from you!" She hustled towards his office.

Earl was silent. Kendra took a deep breath and counted to ten.

"Look, we're supposed to cover these kids together. Can't you at least *try* to help me out?"

Still no answer. She rapped on Earl's door. It swung inward.

Earl's desk was a mess. Spilled coffee had turned sticky and his metal flask was partly visible under a pile of paper. Earl had always kept his desk neat, for all the seventeen months Kendra had been here.

She didn't mean to look out the window; cold fingers seemed to grip her neck and jerk her head up. The lightning flash illuminated something on the far side of the docks. Seagulls circled it.

Kendra's eyes adjusted to the dim, orange light.

Two big gulls fought over a piece of meat. It was pale and thin.

Kendra recognized the anchor tattoo on it, in between the splashes of spray and sheets of rain. She didn't recognize the neon pink slime adhering to it. Something pinkish-white slipped between the planks, beyond the reach of the greedy gulls. As soon as she saw that slip down, her eyes followed the cresting wave. On it was a large white body with the rags of a security uniform. Part of its torso hung open like a hastily peeled orange. A strong current snatched away what remained of Earl.

***

Kendra didn't realize how long she'd been staring until her bad knee buckled. She dropped her cane and caught herself before her face hit the tiled floor.

If she had seen the dreadful sight at home, she would have turned to her stepfather or auntie for confirmation. If she'd been alone, she would have locked the doors and turned on the lights. Even now, her common sense insisted that what she'd seen wasn't real.

She flipped on the walkie-talkie. "101 to 102, please respond." Static. "101 to 102, please respond. Urgent!" Nothing.

She knew better. Her clammy palms and ragged breath and sweat-soaked collar insisted: *somebody* had murdered Earl in a very nasty way. Downstairs, the kids waited unaware.

Kendra touched the cold window glass and saw the rain and hail sticking to it. This was *real*. She walked to the elevator, took deep breaths and stepped in. While the machinery hummed she put on her best fake smile, the one she used to greet ex-girlfriends in the grocery store or homophobic relatives at Thanksgiving.

The elevator doors opened. The kids turned to face her all at once. The wind went silent.

"Are you okay?" Sancho said. He tugged Kendra's sleeve gently. Her thoughts scattered like groceries from a torn bag.

"Just a little winded," Kendra said. Her own voice sounded distant. "Thank you," she added, and pushed her face back into a smile.

Anyone who could take on Earl would outclass her, no contest. He'd been *opened*. Kendra clutched her chest. She needed to protect the kids from whoever waited out there...assuming they weren't in here.

But why would they be out there? Even serial killers didn't like the wet and cold. She'd seen no other vehicles nearby. It was a long trek to the nearest hotel or bar. Her heart beat faster. Her fingers tightened on the cane.

She couldn't call the police. If there'd been a body, bleeding onto the carpet or stuffed into the trash can, that would be one thing; but the police liked quick, easy answers. Kendra had no proof.

Police didn't like "prank calls" and, like vampires, they gained power if you invited them in. *Whatever* could tear something vital out of a beefy security guard and vanish into the night would not be troubled by police. *Whoever,* she corrected herself insistently.

Kendra opened her eyes. Adriana and Thomas argued softly. Sophie discreetly tried to copy Fareeda's paper. Sancho was filling in the edges of his sheet with drawings of flowers. Taylor completed their fourth page with nothing but purple and green.

Hypothetically, it wasn't impossible for a child to kill a full grown man, with the right tools and enough preparation. *Where had that idea come from?* A draft whispered past the back of her neck.

Six children stood before Kendra. The parents had dropped off five children. She had the evidence of her own eyes.

"We're all done!" Thomas shouted suddenly.

Kendra barely stifled her scream.

***

"What do we do next?" Taylor asked. Kendra wondered how many small children had parents who would buy them clothes that didn't conform to a rigid girl or boy theme and let them perform mad science experiments with their hair. Certainly not her own "it's just a phase" birth-parents. Anyway, it was better than exploring her nightmarish epiphany.

"Next?" Kendra said. "Right, next up on the lesson plan." She tried to think. She picked up her printout of the agenda.

Nautical Stargazing: learning how sailors guided themselves with the heavens, with a note about alternatives for bad weather. A voice in her mind whispered that she needed to act like nothing was wrong, or *worse* things would happen. Maybe it was one of the oceanic gods she didn't quite believe in; maybe it was just experience.

She looked out the window. The hail had stopped and the rain settled into a spray rather than an assault. The platform for oyster tonging had an outdoor roof over it. She stepped out under the sheltered roof and motioned the children to follow.

"Does anyone know the history of this building?" Kendra thumped her hand on the reassuring wood. Old oak could be tougher than stone, and more flexible. It was a good thing to have between yourself and a serial killer-haunted night. *You know it's not a serial killer*, her hindbrain whispered.

Kendra pointed to Fareeda's raised hand, overlooking Thomas's jumping up and down and Adriana's frantic wave.

"Um, this was the dock for sailors who caught oysters?" she squeaked.

"Very good," Kendra said. "They used giant tongs to scrape up oysters off the seabed." The orange light made even the shallows look like red wine.

The *Agwe's Hand* smacked against the dock. Kendra helped Sophie into a nautical oilskin. Why did children always have such sticky hands? She stepped up to the barnacle-crusted steel and oak pier.

Kendra gripped the smoothed wooden handles, then levered

the creaking iron tongs. Thomas acted bored while Adriana showed un-ashamed fascination with the giant limbs of steel. Kendra demonstrated, scraping up a pyrite chunk she'd tossed in there earlier with the claw-like tong teeth.

While the kids took their turns, Kendra rummaged around the site. She didn't know exactly what she was looking for.

Nevertheless, she found it.

Tucked into a dark corner, beneath piled nets and life vests, was something like a big lobster shell. It was flexible, like plastic, and hot pink on the inside. Instead of eyestalks and mouthparts, it had a ragged pink hole.

Kendra knew lobsters shed their old shells; this was nothing like that. It looked like a jellyfish's lobster costume. Octopi and sea slugs at-tending a fancy costume ball in the court of *Olokun* danced in her mind's eye. She pinched herself hard.

She didn't want to believe what this floppy lobster suit implied. She'd watched footage of the mimic octopus and she'd seen a remake of *Invasion of the Body Snatchers* on her fourth date with Trisha.

Taylor stared at her as the other kids tried to spot fish in the water or gathered around the tongs. Taylor, who didn't really fit, with hair so spiky-bright. All those temporary tattoos would be easy for something that changed its skin color like a cuttlefish.

She shoved the not-lobster back into the rubbish and waved. Tay-lor stared a while longer, then told Thomas that his turn was over.

But wouldn't a wolf in sheep's clothing try extra hard to look sheepish? It wouldn't stand out like Taylor. *Thomas* looked more like the "normal" kid...

Lightning flashed in the distance. Kendra told herself that this was insane. She couldn't suspect a child of being an amorphous bogeyman. If there was a monster that could change into anything, somebody would have discovered it by now.

Really? she thought, feeling damp chill soak into her bones. *There was a twenty foot shark with jaws you could drive an SUV into and it wasn't discovered until a few decades ago. How long will it take them to find something that survives by looking like other things? What geothermal vent or icy grotto did it crawl out of?*

Kendra squeezed her cane and tried to ground herself in the real world. The kids were staring at her. She scanned their eyes for something inhuman; she just saw nervous kids.

"Are you alright?" Sancho asked, squinting at her name tag, "Ms. Kendra Carpenter?"

"I'm fine," Kendra said, unconsciously wiping her hands. "Has everyone had a turn with the tongs?"

Adriana nodded sadly. The others murmured variations of "yes".

"I think we can start the oyster-shucking then," she said, in an attempt at enthusiasm.

Taylor and Adriana seemed pleased. Sancho and Fareeda were indifferent. Sophie looked back at the tongs. "I didn't get a turn yet," she said.

"Yes you did, liar," Thomas snapped.

"I think she did," Fareeda said, looking down.

Sophie smiled weakly at Thomas. "Can we be friends?"

Thomas snorted and rolled his eyes.

"I'll be your friend," Sancho said, offering Sophie his hand. The kids followed Kendra inside.

Would the imposter be aggressive, like Thomas, or extra-friendly, like Sancho or Sophie? Maybe it would linger in the background, quiet and unobtrusive, like Fareeda. Kendra closed the door behind them and locked it. This made her feel calmer.

She remembered learning that hair was hard to render in CGI, all those different strands moving at once. Maybe the fuchsia creature, the not-lobster, had trouble making hair? It hadn't bothered with an external copy of the eyestalks and mouthparts, so maybe it wasn't a perfect mimic. Would she find something pink and slimy if she pulled off Fareeda's head covering?

Kendra's cane skidded on a plastic wrapper. Fareeda caught it, and she braced herself upright. "Thank you," Kendra said, looking deep into the gentle brown eyes. She hated herself for suspecting the girl. *Maybe the pink imitator would try to act helpful.*

Thunder rolled. Kendra jumped. She kept her balance this time. She almost lost it again when Sophie snapped her bubblegum.

Kendra took the children over to the oyster dissection table. She picked up a dead oyster and the knife. Sophie smiled at her. Adriana smiled at the glint of electric light on the blade. Thomas stepped closer. Taylor cocked her/his/their head. Fareeda folded her hands and watched. Sancho looked squeamish.

Kendra explained how oysters filtered pollution out of the water and told them about the thriving hub of industry this region used to be.

What was she supposed to look for?

Kendra sat. She cut open the oyster with more care and precision than the pink imitator had shown with Earl. Maybe if the pink monster slipped into a staff meeting, she'd be able to spot it. If it pretended to be an adult or somebody familiar, she might have a chance.

"Any questions before we start?" she said. Even her biological mother couldn't have faulted her calm, steady tone. The room stank of ammonia, from the dead oyster or the cleaning supplies. Thunder rolled again.

Fareeda raised her hand.

"Are oysters *halal*?"

Kendra tried to remember details from the Thanksgivings where Aunt Sabine came over. She remembered most things that were kosher were also *halal*, but the rules didn't completely overlap, and vegan stuff was safe for either diet.

"I'm not positive, but we aren't eating these anyway. The pollution they filter out makes these oysters unsafe as food." She wondered if the pink imitator liked pollution-free oysters as much as human organs.

"The good news is, with every generation of oysters, the water gets a bit cleaner, and someday the bay will be good for oyster farming again. Any other questions?"

Sancho raised his dainty hand. "Do these oysters have pearls?"

"Most of these oysters produce small, irregular pearls, nothing jewelry-quality," she ran over the camp rules in her head, "but you can keep any pearls you find."

That sparked interest. Kids going to a nautical camp would expect a treasure hunt.

"Anything else?"

Sophie raised her hand. "Dolphins are intelligent and graceful."

Adriana and Taylor giggled. Thomas rolled his eyes.

"Okay then, let's get started. Remember to always cut *away* from yourself." She passed out the tools and wrote instructions and a diagram on the whiteboard.

Sophie fumbled her knife a bit, but got the hang of it without even looking at the sign. Nobody burst out of their skin. No one pointed and screamed. The children dissected their oysters without stabbing each other. The only extra eyes and mouths were dyed onto Taylor's skin.

Kendra began to doubt that any of these kids was really a slimy changeling. She must have just gotten the roster wrong. As for Earl... well, maybe he had torn his belly open on a jagged piece of metal. Stranger accidents had happened.

Only none of those accidents left fireball-fuchsia slime; and Earl was the kind of man who considered showering without a friction mat dangerous.

So maybe some big scary thing out of cryptozoology had ripped Earl open. That didn't mean it was still here. That didn't mean it had compressed and warped itself into a false form, or drowned some child and crawled inside their skin...

"Okay, who's ready for dinner?" Kendra squeaked. The kids jumped up in assent. She hurried them along a stretch of well-lit pier to the Oyster Pirate's Café.

As they walked, Kendra stepped on a bottle with one foot and a plastic bag with the other. The wet boards hit her like a backhand. Sea spray smacked her bare flabby stomach. For one terrifying moment, she skidded over the edge and stared into rose-colored foam beneath.

She pulled herself back on the planks and dug her nails in, ignoring the splinters. Sophie stared open-mouthed, gum hanging off her tongue. Thomas rushed over and handed her the cane.

"Thank you," she gasped, carefully levering herself to a standing position. "By the way, you might want to watch your step here."

Nervous laughter broke out. Kendra limped into the café just as she remembered that Earl would have prepared the food.

She showed the kids how to make a traditional oyster habitat out of recycled materials, then turned on the ovens. Cooking helped her calm down. She pulled mussels and shrimps out of the fridge, then greased a pan with olive oil. Sautéed mushrooms would add some texture to the vegan seaweed salad. Fareeda would appreciate that.

Kendra didn't think Fareeda could possibly be a sea monster. How would it learn about Islamic dietary law? Then again, how would the pink imitator learn to speak at all?

There was a tall lager in the fridge. Never mind who left it there, never mind that it was against the rules. Kendra used a parrot-shaped bottle opener and chugged the beer. She *needed* this, medically.

She ducked over to the windows and confirmed that the kids were building. Thomas was making the biggest habitat. Sophie looked at everyone else before adding her melted bottles to the sides. No one ripped anyone's face off.

Kendra's stomach churned. Sweat ran down her back. Maybe the pink sea monster was full. One full-grown man's internal organs might be enough. Maybe it just needed some special nutrient. Maybe it would leave the others in peace.

She ducked away from the window and turned to the shrimp. The Captain Picker's Shellfish Sauce reminded her of the foam under the pier.

Kendra's memory jolted into perfect recall. The foam had been bundled—tethered almost—against one pillar. She recalled the twisting pink shapes in it, with miniscule eyestalks or tentacles over things that might be fins or claws. *Didn't some creatures become ravenous and aggressive around breeding season?*

Kendra pulled the mushrooms from the pan before they burned. She tossed the seaweed salad and grabbed a pack of Sunshine Vegan

Cookies. She clipped the plate onto her cane and tottered over to Fareeda.

"I'm sorry about the delay. Good work everyone. All those nooks and crannies will provide a place for juvenile oysters to grow. The other meals will be out soon." She paused for breath.

Fareeda looked up. Kendra saw her own mad terror reflected in the girl's knowing brown eyes.

"You're not really okay, are you?" Fareeda whispered.

"No," Kendra said. "I'm not."

The lights died. Another roll of thunder hit. Everyone screamed.

***

"Everyone stay calm!" Kendra said. Their screams increased. "The back-up generator will come on in a few seconds."

Somebody slammed into her. She heard a wet, tearing sound. Adriana had a blue LED flashlight, but it shook so much it only added to the confusion. Kendra saw a flash of pink and a spray of red. The flashlight bounced on the floor.

The generator kicked in. Blood was everywhere. It sprayed from Adriana. Her eyes were rolled back. Something had ripped off her shirt and...

The terror inside Kendra froze.

"Everyone, get back!" she shouted. She pushed away the kids who didn't move quick enough, forcing Thomas and Sophie onto their butts. The thought that she might get fired for such brutality bounced off her skull.

"Don't touch her!" Kendra's cane rapped against the floor. She swung open the medicine cabinet and yanked down the first aid kit. She noticed that the jar of shark liver oil pills lay empty on its side.

She rushed back, ignoring her throbbing leg.

The kids had clustered together. That was dangerous.

"Get away from each other! Stand back."

They separated. Kendra squeezed Adriana's hand. "Can you hear me?"

Adriana groaned and coughed. The flesh was torn back just above her stomach. It wasn't bleeding as bad as it could be.

"You're very brave. This will hurt. I'm sorry," Kendra did her best to seal the wound and dialed 911 on her cell. "Bayside Discovery Project, kid here nearly got her liver ripped out. Send help." She tossed the phone away and ignored it ringing. She applied disinfectant with a generous hand. Who knew what noxious bacteria had been dredged up from the deep?

Once she had done all she could for Adriana—*please Poseidon, Agwe, Aegir, Olokun, Mazu, if any of you exist please don't let her die on my watch*—Kendra looked at the other kids. Sancho knelt down, crying "Princess unicorn help us!" Thomas sniffled and pounded his fist on the table. Taylor was curled in a ball. Fareeda had closed her eyes and clutched her hands and was whispering urgently. Sophie shivered and chewed her gum.

"Spell your names," Kendra said. The children stared at her.

She didn't have a gun. She didn't know if a knife would be any good. Nobody had thought to provide the Bayside Discovery Project with cattle prods or flamethrowers.

She strode towards the kitchen. "Sancho, spell your name."

Sancho looked up at her. "What?"

"Just spell your name for me, please," she said, not slowing down.

"S-A-N-C-H-O," he said as Kendra entered the kitchen.

"Good. Now get Adriana a blanket and a pillow, and don't let anyone else near her." Sancho rushed to obey. "Fareeda, your turn."

Kendra grabbed the fire extinguisher. The kitchen also had a stash of back-up fuel for the generator. She stuffed a canister in her pocket. Fareeda spelled her name.

Kendra turned to Taylor. "Just spell your name."

"My name is Taylor," the child said, eyes wide and unfocused.

"I know. Now, please, spell it."

"I…I just…my," they stammered, eyes wide and pleading. They stuck out a finger and sketched the letter "T" in the air, biting their lip.

"You're okay," Kendra said. She hadn't realized the kid was neurodivergent.

She turned to Sophie. "Spell your name for me, please."

Sophie was still crying. She shuffled her feet. "I'm Sophie and I have a puppy."

"I know that, Sophie, now spell your damn name." Kendra

emerged from the kitchen, most of her weight on the cane, hiding the fire extinguisher behind her back.

Sophie trembled.

"Everyone who's human, step away from her, carefully," Kendra said in a soothing tone. The other kids edged away. Sophie looked at them before shuffling backwards.

"Sophie, are you dyslexic?" Kendra asked, her face blank.

Sophie edged away from the table, toward the door. Something in her gurgled. "Can we be friends?"

Kendra just watched her.

Sophie scrunched up her face and waved her hands. "Get lost!"

"I just want you to spell your name. Or write it. Or just try to explain why you can't. Use some words that you didn't pick up from the documentary playing on a loop in the main lobby. Tell me something you didn't just copy from somebody else." Kendra lost the fight to keep her voice calm.

Fareeda moved towards her. "It's okay…Sophie. Nobody wants to hurt you."

Sophie blew a big bubble, which burst. Two strands of darker pink lashed against Fareeda's face. Kendra lunged toward Sophie as blue light crackled between Sophie's tentacles. Fareeda fell to the ground, twitching and gasping for breath.

Kendra grabbed Fareeda, sucked the wound and spat in case any venom had lodged there. Sophie foamed and swayed, making a rubbery noise. The other children were too scared to move.

Kendra tried to stomp on the long pink tendrils, but they retracted too quickly. Sophie was already thinner and taller. Bulges seethed under the clothes that melted into her skin. Kendra sprayed the fire extinguisher, filling the doorway with cold hissing foam, then swung the extinguisher hard at Sophie's head.

Its head cracked. Vermillion slime squirted from its ears and nose. The creature stayed upright as the deflated mass sagged. It didn't keep its brain there.

Thomas flung cutlery at it. The monster lurched towards him.

Kendra yanked the fuel container from her pocket. The thing lashed its tentacles at her. For seconds she couldn't breathe, couldn't move. Burnt hair stank in her nose. Blue light flickered at the edge of vision, but most of the sparks ran down her cane.

Kendra fell and gasped as not-Sophie retracted its tentacles. It reared up and opened a five-fanged mouth on its left foot. The horror kicked at Thomas. He ducked the first swing, but it popped another joint into existence and bit him on the neck. Taylor pulled off their spiky belt and whipped the pink creature until it let go.

Kendra dumped the can of gas on it. Its pink flesh blistered and sizzled. It screamed and sprang backwards. The firm limbs went boneless and flaccid. It mewled and whined, trying to spit out the toxin that had slipped into its orifices. A set of gills bulged at its neck. A claw sticking out of its thigh dripped with grease. The creature lay still.

***

Kendra prodded the corpse twice, then checked on Fareeda. The girl's eyes didn't focus, and she was moaning, but her breathing and heart rate seemed regular. She'd suffered no more than a superficial electrical burn.

"She'll be okay," Sancho insisted. "My big brother got hit with a police stun gun. It hurts a lot, but you get better."

"Yes, I think it's like that," Kendra said. She patted Sancho on the shoulder. "You stay here with her. I'll be right back."

Kendra sanitized and bandaged up Thomas's neck. He took it like a real trooper. Taylor changed Adriana's bandages. Then Kendra marched outside.

She grabbed some big hooks, weights and nets from the working demonstration cabinet. She returned to the room, sweating under the weight. She drove a hook into each of the dead pink monster's limbs. Fareeda, sitting up now, cheered along with Sancho and Taylor. Thomas glared at it.

Once Kendra was sure it was really, truly dead, she handed out plastic gloves. She beckoned to Thomas and gave him a pike to drive in. He screamed as he stabbed the corpse, then slumped to the floor and started crying. Sancho smashed the Sophie-thing's claw with an iron ballast.

Kendra stumbled over when Adriana coughed. The little girl, pale as death, said her tummy hurt, and wanted to know if her oyster habitat was okay.

"It's perfect," Kendra said. "Help is on the way." She paused. "Do you want anything?"

Adriana gasped. "Some special mommy water? I'm not allowed to share, but I always wondered."

Kendra considered that a possible last request outweighed the drinking age. She offered Earl's flask to Adriana; the girl choked down a sip.

Fareeda prayed to the Abrahamic God and Sancho called to his unicorn princess. Thomas just cried a lot. Adriana faded in and out of consciousness. Everyone took turns squeezing her hand. She asked for a juice box and a cookie but didn't wake up to enjoy them.

Taylor walked up to Kendra while the others discussed people, fictional and real, who had almost died.

"Was Sophie…a humanoid from the deep?" Taylor whispered.

"Something like that," Kendra said, with a shrug. "I'll have to suck up the eggs it laid with a wet vac, then see if anyone at the university knows what to do with them. If I'm lucky the white scientists won't get all the credit for our discovery." She bit her lip. She was rambling.

Taylor frowned, uncomprehending. Sirens rang in the air.

Kendra opened the door for the EMTs. She shoved them past the mutilated sea monster. As the experts hooked up an IV of blood to Adriana, they told Kendra that she'd prevented shock from setting in. She would need to look up every kind of ritual thanks-offering to briny deities the moment she returned home.

Taylor tugged on her hand.

"Ms. Kendra? I just want to thank you for not calling me a boy or a girl. Also, I can't wait to come back next year!"

My Dad used to be a magician; he was
in the Guinness Book for card throwing.
He [would] throw playing cards at my sister
and me when we'd get into trouble.
I grew up watching him cut my Mom in half...

Michelle Lodge

DISPOSABLE

I think of all the garbage
that humans have created,
and it's overwhelming.

I also feel culpable.
I'm a part of the human race
who creates garbage and expects it
to disappear when the truck hauls it away.
It's only a matter of time before
we have to deal with it in a real way...

Our garbage will eventually kill us,
both literally and figuratively.
[And] the Earth would be better for it.

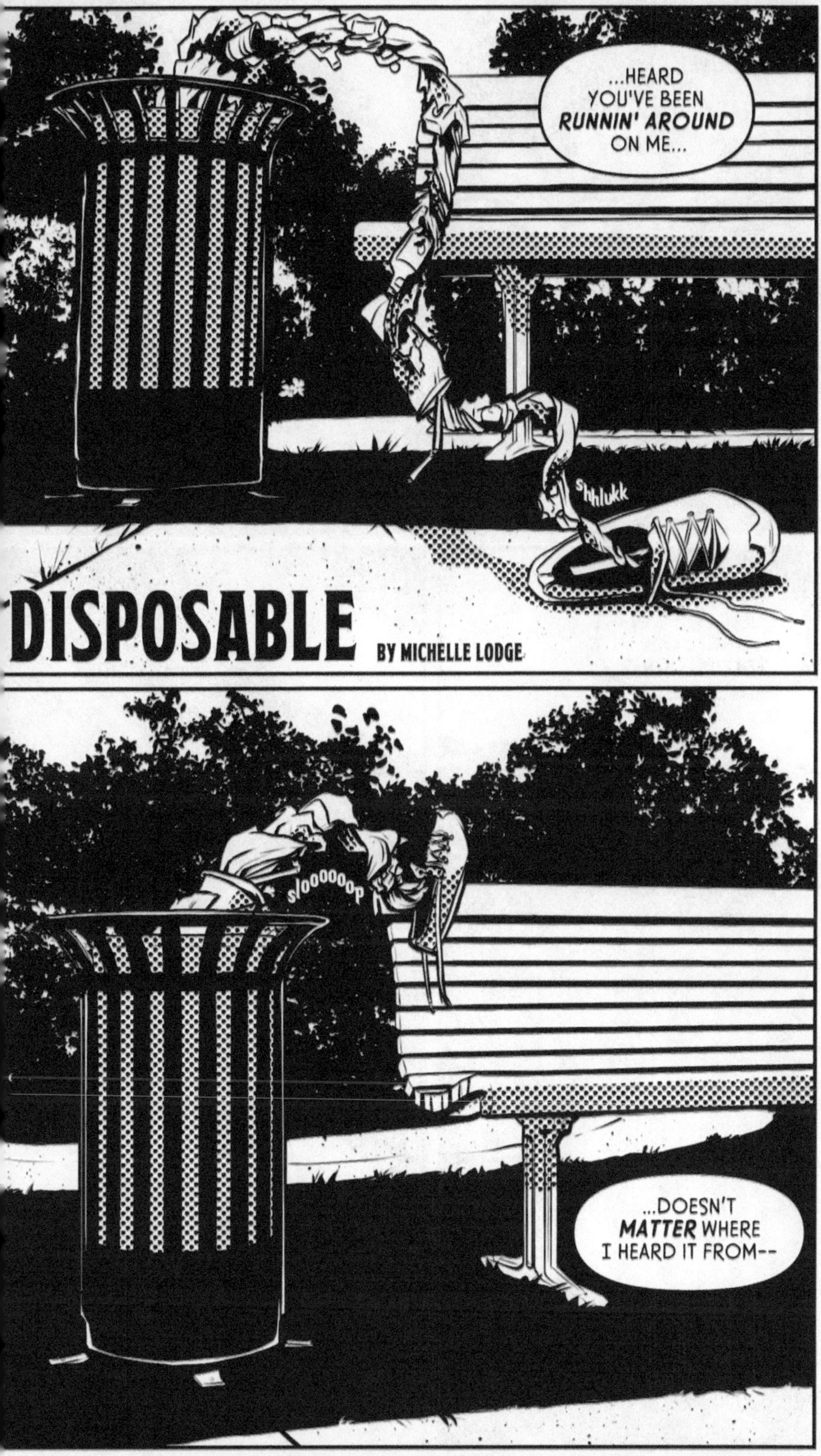

DISPOSABLE

BY MICHELLE LODGE

ARE YOU SERIOUSLY CALLING ME CRAZY?
ME?
...HUH. WELL, GUESS YOU CAN CHANGE YOUR STATUS, THEN—

A LIE? TELL YA WHAT, I KNOW A LIE WHEN I HEAR ONE. LIKE NOW. I HEAR—

BOOP-!
...

...WHATEVER.

SSSSSSSSSSSSHHHH

SSHHSSSH
URBL
LBURBLBURBLBU

SPLORCH

GAH-!
WH-WHA THE HELL-
W-WAIT-!

LEMME GO—
HN... WHA—
NO! NOOOO—

...

END.

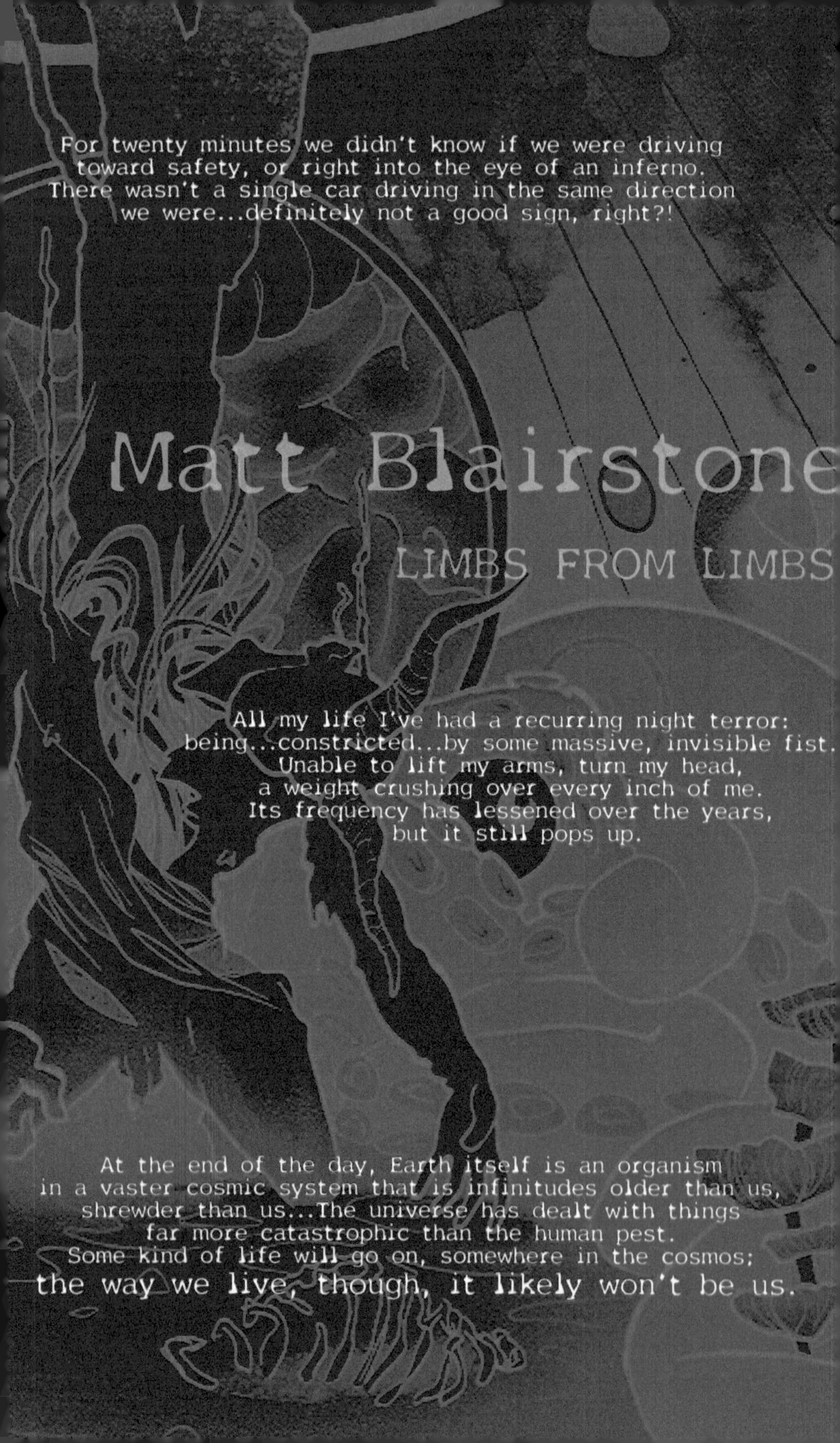

For twenty minutes we didn't know if we were driving
toward safety, or right into the eye of an inferno.
There wasn't a single car driving in the same direction
we were...definitely not a good sign, right?!

Matt Blairstone

LIMBS FROM LIMBS

All my life I've had a recurring night terror:
being...constricted...by some massive, invisible fist.
Unable to lift my arms, turn my head,
a weight crushing over every inch of me.
Its frequency has lessened over the years,
but it still pops up.

At the end of the day, Earth itself is an organism
in a vaster cosmic system that is infinitudes older than us,
shrewder than us...The universe has dealt with things
far more catastrophic than the human pest.
Some kind of life will go on, somewhere in the cosmos;
the way we live, though, it likely won't be us.

LIMBS FROM LIMBS
BY MATT BLAIRSTONE

A squat thing crept from the catacombs of Maria's psyche on fat misshapen toes. It slouched alongside her as she peeked through slitted curtains, watching her husband Cam talk to the police officer outside. The squat thing was *Dread* and on the rare occasion it emerged, it was near impossible to convince it to return to its pestilential cage in any kind of timely manner. *Dread* adhered to its own devices; sometimes the fractured hands of its dubious timepiece seemed frozen in time.

Now, in a bedroom illuminated only by shafts of yellow light that streamed between the curtains, *Dread* pressed its gray fingers to the low curve of Maria's back, sending a queasy snake of sweat wriggling up her spine. She loathed not being able to hear her husband's conversation with the cop outside. Inside the rental house, the only sound was the howling wind and Valentina's relentless jabbering from the other room as she played Miss Piggy tea party.

At last Cam trotted back to the house, fidgeting with the mask that covered his mouth and nose. The cop's SUV crawled away down the narrow road, its looped evacuation warning blasting from a roof-mounted speaker. The strobing emergency lights collided with the smoky yellow that draped the world, like an incursion of neon into the sepia tint of a silent film. Maria let the curtains fall from her fingers and left the bedroom, refusing to acknowledge *Dread* as it tagged along, clinging to the belt loop of her jeans.

"What did he say?" she asked, meeting Cam as he closed the front door behind him. The smoke that had wafted in hung in the entryway. Behind Maria, Valentina poured banana tea for Kermie and Gonzo.

"It's getting worse out there," Cam said, pulling the mask from his face. "Like holding your face over a campfire. That *color* is definitely messing with my eyes."

He pinched the bridge of his nose, either to exaggerate his discomfort or because he was genuinely disoriented, Maria didn't know which. Cam looked both wide awake and sleep-deprived at the same time, which was fair. Maria had woken early herself, only to find that her husband had risen before the sun and was packing their belongings in the dark. He'd gotten a glimpse at what the world outside looked like, he'd told her, and knew then and there that they wouldn't be staying the two remaining nights of their reservation. Maria wasn't upset about not being consulted;

it was the right call.

"What did the cop say?" she repeated, trying to mask her agitation. *Dread* had scaled her spine and was squiggling an oily slug of a finger along her neck, where her black hair was bound in a hasty bun. She resisted the urge to swat the invasive digit away.

"They're evacuating everyone," Cam replied. "Wind is pushing the wildfires faster than anyone can keep up with. Sounds like *everything* to the immediate east of here went up in flames. We gotta get gone, quick."

"What about the roads? If we can't go east-"

"*Hedro,* I think? That town ring a bell? *Drive to Hedro,* the cop said. Said it's north of here, but I can't verify that with the Wi-Fi down. My phone maps won't even load. Is yours…?"

"Nothing," Maria replied, "and it's nearly dead anyway. I'm at five percent." The power in most of the little beach town had been out since yesterday, the morning after their first night in the rental, so of course none of their devices were charged. The extraordinary winds had snapped power lines and spread the southern wildfires right to their doorstep.

She patted her own phone in her pocket, taking scant relief in its presence. *Dread* sent electrical arcs racing along her jawline, making her fillings tingle. A bubble of acid scaled her esophagus; she swallowed it down with a grimace.

"Alright," Cam said, "I'm gonna do a quick look around, make sure we didn't miss anything. Can you pack up Val's bag?"

Maria was already scooping up Valentina's plastic teacups as Cam prowled the lightless house, searching for anything forgotten, swinging the flashlight on his phone so erratically that Maria knew his efforts would be fruitless. Val squealed and flailed at having her playtime interrupted.

"Sorry baby," Maria cooed, "you can watch Daniel Tiger once we're in the car." The little girl fell silent.

Cam grabbed his wallet and keys off the dinner table. Maria was quietly impressed; the typical politics of their relationship dictated that she was president and he vice. *Or queen and court jester,* he liked to joke. It worked well for them, most of the time.

His sudden decisiveness almost helped her ignore *Dread* weighing on her shoulders like a pack laden with stones. Almost.

"Got everything?" Cam squeezed her shoulder. "Let's go."

Flakes of ash drifted from the sky as Maria carried Valentina to her car seat.

***

Their lack of familiarity with the area gifted *Dread's* intrusive fingers an angry set of talons that seared into Maria's neck as they neared the main drag. Traffic was at a standstill, extending southbound as far as she could see, crossing in front of them and continuing for a couple hundred yards before the line terminated. More headlights were lining up in the queue, but the smoke was too thick to see beyond that.

South, not north. Despite what the cop had told Cam, everyone else was driving south. The northbound lane, the direction Cam thought

Hedro was, sat empty.

What do they know that we don't? Maria scanned the vehicles in front of them. A young man and woman, garbed in matching blue windbreakers, gabbed mutely inside their Subaru Outback; each of them fiddled with phones that were likely as useless as Cam's and her own were. Behind the Subaru loomed a massive black Silverado, a broad bearded man in a trucker's hat drumming his fingers along the steering wheel. A decal on the rear side panel of the truck caught her eye; *I Will Not Comply,* it read, over an illustration of a surgical mask. Fresh pricks of *Dread,* then, in the sensitive flesh where her ear met her skull.

As the Silverado crept forward, she saw another bumper sticker below the license plate: *Fear Is The Real Killer. Dread* wheezed sandpaper laughter in her ear.

She realized Cam had been talking for a bit. "Sorry, I was somewhere else," she said.

Annoyed, Cam started again. "I said, I'm not gonna pretend I know what the hell I'm talking about, but the cop said Hedro is a couple miles north of here. He said the eastbound near Hedro was—*as far as he knew*—still open. That it was our best bet to get out of this area. But…"

He gestured at the wall of traffic heading south.

"Yeah," Maria mumbled. *"But."*

"So," said Cam, "we *could* go south…I mean, everyone else is. Or do we trust that Officer Friendly knows what he's talkin' about?"

Maria glanced back at Val in her car seat. The girl was oblivious to their turmoil. Oversized headphones covered her ears. The iPad was pressed too closely to her wide eyes as she absorbed Daniel Tiger's important lesson about being patient.

"Trust has nothing to do with it," Maria said. "Shit, Cam, I have no idea. It's not like taking the wrong route and being late for a dinner reservation. This is potentially driving into an *inferno*."

The line of traffic had grown at least a quarter mile longer as they had dithered, with little movement. *Dread* scraped a jagged line along the inside of Maria's throat; she struggled not to gag on its noxious taste.

"Alright. Let's try north," she said.

That was all Cam needed. The tires squealed as he swerved through a narrow gap in the stalled line of vehicles and drove north. The thick smoke gave no clue as to the rightness of their decision; it enveloped everything, everywhere.

***

Dread tried to appropriate Maria's body a few times over the next half hour, but each time she tamped it down. She was reinvigorated when she spotted a pair of northbound cars through the smoke ahead of them. When Cam told her he saw headlights in the rearview too, trailing them through the gloom, it lifted her spirits further, and she was able to kneecap *Dread* into begrudging silence for a while longer. It was proof of nothing, *meant* nothing except they weren't the only idiots driving north. That realization brought more relief than she'd anticipated.

When we drive into a wall of fire at sixty miles an hour, at least we'll have company, she thought. It brought a curl of a smile to her lips. Then she saw lights ahead, flashing jewels piercing the septic yellow expanse, and *Dread* lashed the smirk from her face.

"What's that?" she asked. Cam frowned and slowed but said nothing.

A pair of police cruisers were angled to obstruct anyone from turning onto a narrow, unmarked road to the right. Two officers huddled beside their cars. Cam stopped and Maria lowered her window. If anything, the wind had gotten worse; it sounded like the crash of waves. She struggled not to breathe in the smoke that slashed through the open window.

One of the cops was tugging what looked like vines from the rear tires of his cruiser. Maria thought it odd but dismissed it as the other officer approached them. He was already waving them on before Maria had opened her mouth. A mask covered his lower face; Maria could see that his eyes were crimson and tired.

Through a brief exchange she gleaned that continuing north was the only safe option at this point. The officer was noncommittal about any town called Hedro; he just kept waving his arm like a little league coach guiding his runner home. As she rolled up the window, trapping the campfire smell inside the car with them, Maria wondered if the cop had heard a word she'd said.

As Cam drove away, Maria became aware just how dense the forest was around them. The trees towered high, less than twenty feet away, but the smoke was so thick their tops were invisible. She felt lost in the cursed bog of a children's story.

"Slow down, Cam," she said, squinting to see the trees. She *needed* to see them, to know for a fact that she hadn't been whisked off to some desolate, wasted dream-realm where mighty *Dread* held sway.

"Slow down," she repeated, "you can't see anything."

Cam grunted, but Maria felt the car slow a little. She no longer saw tail lights ahead, nor headlights behind. The flashing red and blue of the cop cruisers had been swallowed by the leviathan of smoke. They were alone.

Dread commandeered her eyes, her ears, her nose, flooding her senses with the ruins of a burning world.

***

They drove another twenty minutes, aware that the ocean was a quarter mile to their west but never once seeing it. The smoke thinned intermittently and Maria would think that the worst was past, but inevitably the yellow miasma would return and swallow them afresh.

She turned in her seat and drummed on Val's foot, desperate for the smothering attention that only a toddler could demand, but the girl only had eyes for Daniel Tiger. It was probably for the best; if Valentina tapped into Maria's naked anxieties, it would only amplify the tension already churning within the car.

"Look at that," Cam said abruptly. "Holy shit, what is *that*?"

Maria looked where he pointed through the windshield. At first there was nothing beyond the uniform unpleasantness of the landscape, but she quickly saw what Cam was singling out: a small clearing, east of the road. The clearing was draped in the same oppressive smoke, but beneath it blazed acid green, so detached from its surroundings that it seemed to glow.

They halted beside the clearing and stared in silence until Valentina, roused from her video when the car had stopped, asked, "Are we there, Mommy?"

Are we where, *honey,* she thought but didn't say, instead uttered, "Not yet baby, not yet…Cam, what is…is it a *sculpture*, do you think? Some kind of art installation?"

"Out *here*?" He laughed humorlessly. "I mean, it's Oregon, so… sure, art installation, why not? Anything's possible. But…why is it glowing?"

"I don't think it's glowing," Maria answered, pressing her face to the window, "it's just so *bright*." She strained to absorb the details of the vignette splayed before them. Twenty yards away the forest resumed, but between the road and the treeline were wildgrass and low plants, brilliant and unnaturally green.

In the middle of the clearing was a bicycle. The front half of it was draped in lichen, spreading from the handlebars to the center of the frame. The front tire was completely encrusted in radiant vegetation, every spoke a splendid shaft of green. The back of the bicycle was less affected, but

Maria could see an array of slender vines were already twining their way through the rear tire and around the pedals. The bike was aimed due east and stood upright, held in place by the tautness of the plants.

Between their car and the bicycle, the ground bulged unevenly; it rose and fell like a mountain range rendered in miniature. It was the same resplendent green, though Maria could see scattered spots of forest floor peeking through the grass.

She was so captivated that she didn't notice when the car engine turned off; the enchantment was only broken when Cam opened his door. She snapped her head around to see him pulling his mask up over his face and exiting the car.

"What are you *doing?*" she said, shrill enough that Valentina looked up in alarm.

Cam held his hands wide, placatory. "I'm just gonna go look. I mean, *that's weird*, right? You gotta admit that's wei-"

"We need to keep going, Cam, I'm serious-"

"Thirty seconds! I'll be right back." He shut the door, crossed in front of the car and crouched beside the bike.

"Goddammit, Cam…" Maria seethed. *Dread* had been doing a stilettoed tap dance on her shoulders, but now white-hot *fury* threatened to thump *Dread* right off the dancefloor.

"Where's Daddy going?" Valentina sounded anxious; Daniel Tiger's spell had been broken.

"He'll be right back, sweetie, don't worry," Maria said, trying to sound calm and failing miserably. She hissed as Cam nosed around the bicycle. "No, don't touch it, you idiot…"

Suddenly, her husband fell backward onto his ass, as though he'd been pushed. Maria gasped as *Dread* spiked a crude lancet through her forehead. Cam scooted backward, away from the bicycle. His left hand touched down on a raised mound of grass. Maria could see her husband's face as he stared down at his hand, his mouth working frantically beneath the mask, his chest rising and falling. The mask hid much of his features, but it couldn't hide that his typical stoicism had been replaced by raw terror.

Yet still he stared spellbound at the misshapen earth. Maria opened the car door an inch.

"Cam!" she snapped, unconcerned with upsetting Valentina. Cam just hovered there on hands and knees, staring at the grass like a confused dog. *Dread's* needle, having made such an intimate home between her eyes, became an icepick and threatened to halve her skull.

"*Cam!*" Now his head snapped up. Their eyes met. "*Get in the goddamn car right now!*"

He was sluggish, stirred from a daze. Finally he clambered to his feet and ran to the driver's side without looking back.

"What was it?" Maria stared hard at her husband as he fumbled with the ignition. Beads of sweat dotted his brow. "What did you *see?*" Cam said nothing. He wrenched the steering wheel to the left and screeched back onto the highway.

Maria frowned at the bicycle as they left it behind. Though it had surely been a trick of the smoke, she thought its front wheel was revolving.

***

They drove for a couple of miles--faster than Maria would've liked, given the lack of visibility, though she said nothing--before Cam finally spoke. He glanced in the rearview to see that Valentina was preoccupied, then said simply,

"There was an ear."

Maria stared at him. After a moment, he continued.

"On the ground. No…*in* the ground…Hold on, I'm not explaining it well, I…it-"

"Hey. *Hey,*" Maria said, squeezing his shoulder. "Just breathe. Put your head in order, take your time." She rarely saw her husband discombobulated, much less on the verge of a panic attack. The sight unnerved her.

Dread is not monogamous, it whispered. She swatted the greedy, greasy wasp away.

"In the ground," Cam began again. "I felt something between my fingers…something that wasn't…*right.*"

He shuddered.

"An ear, Maria. A person's ear. I think the mounds in the grass… I think it was a *person.* Or…maybe, *used* to be a person."

"You mean someone *buried* there? A body?"

"Not buried," Cam said. "No. There were patches of dirt, right? Among the grass. And some places—like where I put my hand down—the dirt…*became* something else. Maybe it was a person *before,* but…whatever I touched, the land had *changed* it. Like the bicycle."

"It was covered in moss or something, right?"

"The bike wasn't *covered* in anything," Cam said, and looked at her. His eyes were wide, but his breathing had slowed. "I touched the frame; *metal,* right? Titanium, aluminum, whatever bikes are made of? Well, I slid my hand up, to where I thought the moss was growing…*on* the bike, but…it wasn't growing on it. It *was* the bike. The front half of the bike…*became moss.*"

"That…Cam, hon, that doesn't make any sense," Maria said. "Look, this whole thing is just…it's *really* messed up, and I know that you-"

"*Goddammit,* Maria, I *saw* it! It wasn't metal anymore! It was… *spongy.* The frame caved in when I touched it." He held his hand for her to see, as if showing it to her proved something.

"What makes something like that happen, Maria? A chemical fire? I dunno, but I'm tellin' you, the back half was a perfectly normal bicycle, and then it just…transformed. It was *vegetation* and…and it was *moving.* Trying to pull itself forward, like it was *fleeing.* I felt it. The moss was crawling, making the bike move…"

Maria looked at the streak of lichen etched across his palm and thought about the tire she had seen turning. She took his hand in her own and smeared her thumb across, trying to wipe the green away. It held fast. Seemed a part of the skin. As if it always had been. Cam watched her. He looked frightened. He pulled his hand away and curled it in a fist, as if hiding it could make it unhappen.

They drove in silence for a while. Her head no longer throbbed but *Dread* was there, coating her tongue in copper, and something else. Pungent, like sour milk.

She looked out the windshield. Her eyes informed her that yes, the air was still toxic with smoke and ash. Yellow and wasted and vaporous. And yet…

Maria sniffed hesitantly.

"Cam," she asked, "do you smell smoke still?"

He rolled his eyes impatiently. "What? Yeah. Of course, I mean, *look* out there-"

"No. I mean, yeah obviously I *see the smoke*. But...do you *smell* it?"

He frowned at her, then he inhaled through his nose and held it. He exhaled, confused.

"I don't…" he began, and looked around the car, as though an answer might present itself.

"That's not smoke," Maria said. "Honestly...it smells like the inside of the compost bin when we don't hose it out. Like wet, rotting vegetables."

Cam opened the window a few inches and pressed his nose to the opening. He gagged immediately.

"*Urghk,*" he coughed, "it's goddamn *foul.*"

"Marsh gas, maybe?" she asked.

"*Marsh gas?* What, are you a botanist now?" Cam said. He grinned tiredly; the car ride had aged him. He kept lifting his blemished hand from the steering wheel and glancing at it.

"Well you're the one theorizing about *chemical fires,* Mr. Wizard. Anyway, I'm serious. It smells like rotten eggs."

Cam nodded. "Where's it coming from, d'you think? Is this just some fresh new hell we have to-"

"*Jesus christ Cam look out!*" Maria screamed. Though hazy, the road had looked straight moments ago. Now a cascade of green swept across the highway, thirty yards in front of them, a churning groundswell of earth tearing over the west embankment, rending through asphalt and logic.

Cam stomped on the brakes, swerving to avoid the heaving earth-wave threatening to crash over them. Maria turned toward the backseat, as if she could do anything for Valentina at this point. The little girl had dropped the iPad and was gaping through saucer eyes as a green wave stampeded up and over the embankment, its shadow already darkening them.

"*It's okay baby it's okay it's okay...*" Maria wrapped her fingers around Val's knee, the only part of her daughter she could reach. She was overwhelmed by sound: the shrill shriek of the failing car brakes, the earth itself roaring like a turbine as it lurched around them. The car groaned; their forward motion terminated abruptly. The back of Maria's head *thwacked* against the windshield. The last thing she saw before she blacked out, filling every window, was green.

***

Cam pulled foil-wrapped salmon filets from the coals and plunked them onto a plate. He carried them into the small kitchen of the rental home, blowing theatrically on his singed fingers and muttering with good humor. He set the plate down, warning Val not to touch it lest she burn her fingers as well.

Maria peeled back the foil to reveal the salmon, perfectly cooked. Steam billowed out. The smoky aroma was dizzying.

Cam kissed her forehead, kissed Val. Maria smiled. Outside the sun was horizon-bound, kissing the ocean, painting the sky crimson and orange. This getaway was precisely what they'd needed, she knew; to re-set everything, the tensions of this ruinous year, to wash it clean and start anew. She felt hope for the first time in ages...

...but *Dread* was never far; steadfast comrade *Dread*, sinking its claws into the cavities of Maria's skull as her eyes landed on the sheared expanse of Douglas fir that had smashed through the windshield and pulverized the driver's seat headrest, occupying the space where Cam's head should be. Her husband's neck ended in a pulpy, sinewy mess of red and pink, blood and bone; headless, his body clung white-knuckled to the steering wheel, defying the physics of it all, sharing with his wife one last glimpse at his gallows humor.

In another world, this would have been *Dread's coup de grace,* its chill fingers guiding Maria down a rickety flume of delirium from which she might never rise. Instead, the concordance of distress surrounding her—behind, where Valentina was shrieking; above, where a rain of blows pounded on the roof of the car—served as a centering influence. Maria looked long enough at Cam's decapitated body to recognize it for what it was—a desecrated sack of meat, no longer her husband—and flung her door open.

She couldn't understand what she was seeing at first. An acid green cascade stampeded across the car; a topiary herd become sentient, imprecise hooves clattering and fumbling on legs that didn't know how to be legs. The herd smashed its hastily assimilated bodies against the metal, clumsy, wild. Pieces of the green cascade attempted to fuse with the car itself, while others scrambled away in the meat of deer bodies they had only just begun to master.

Finally the pelting hoofbeats thinned and quieted. Maria peeked from the car and saw that the migration had passed. She opened Valentina's door. One of Val's shoulder straps had twisted and jammed. As Maria tried to muscle it loose she saw a creep of movement out of the corner of her eye.

Slender strands of moss snaked into the car through the shattered windshield, crawling up her husband's arm to the gory crater atop his body. The tree that had pierced the car bled thick amber sap; it beaded up to the tree's skin and oozed toward Cam's body. Maria couldn't tear her gaze away as sap bled into the wound.

At last Val's strap loosened. Maria pulled her daughter from the car seat as Cam's headless body began to convulse.

Val began to whimper. Maria pulled the girl to her, shielding her view of the corpse as it spasmed against its seatbelt. She slammed the car door and turned to flee, Val cradled to her chest, but stopped as she saw the magnitude of what was happening around her.

The forest was roiling. It trembled and thrummed and lurched. Trees strained against their primeval roots. Wild spike-rush grasses seethed to a rhythm independent of the searing winds.

Knotweed married with the decayed remains of a coyote pup and taught itself to walk anew on stunted legs of muscle and sinew and pinkish white flowers. Everywhere Maria looked, the green of the world was tapping into flesh and blood and machine, teaching itself to move, move *faster, escape, assimilate.* Refashioning its slow collective will into something cunning.

Maria lifted her foot away as a brilliant orange tiger lily twined its stem around her ankle. The ground beneath her rippled and she fell; Val nearly spilled from her arms. There was a clatter of metal and glass behind her. She turned to see Cam's headless body positively *flailing* in the driver's seat, injected with a surge of reanimation. Vines and grasses devoured the car around him, *becoming* the wheels, forcing themselves to creak forward.

Dread took over, declared ownership, changed the locks and painted the walls yellow. There was no telling where the smoke was coming from, where the fire was nearest. Maria and her daughter could not stay; the very air queased with evil heat.

The trees dragged their roots toward the east. Maria dove through vine maples that lunged drunkenly; she leapt over weeds that tugged at her legs. Deeper into the woods she ran, where the shuddering of leaves and the growling of ancient timber contorting in ways it had never attempted were so deafening that even the wind was drowned out.

A low blackberry vine snarled around her ankle. She fell again, shielding Val as best she could. A broken branch gouged her cheek; *deep*, she knew immediately. Crimson drops spattered on the plum-hued leaves of a plant she couldn't identify.

Electricity rocketed up Maria's leg. She howled and looked down; the thorns of the blackberry vine sliced into her calf. In moments the vine had snaked beneath her skin. She could see its imprint bulging taut against the inside of her flesh, each scrape of the thorns bringing fresh starbursts of pain. Clutching Val with one hand, she struggled to claw her way along the forest floor, but it was useless; the vine had her snared, and there were more besides.

All around her, the forest sensed that a new carriage had arrived, a thing with *muscle,* with *legs,* a thing that *runs, escapes the flames,* a chariot that could hie east, east, *east.* The forest swarmed; it needed her, demanded her speed.

Maria saw the vine beneath her flesh—already it had wound its way up to her thigh—pulsating with the same acid green. Glowing. *Cam was right, it* is *glowing.* The blood dripping from her cheek was no longer red, but green.

Valentina squirmed in her arms. "Sss'oohhhkay..." Maria said, her tongue no longer her own, but a strange bulbous tuber inside the meat of her head; her words were garbled as they tumbled from the bruised petals of her lips.

Please leave my baby girl be, this carriage of meat pleaded, *leave her be leave her be leave her beeee...*

The green did not respond, held no desire for dialogue. Communion was not its goal, only assimilation. Escape. *Dread* fueled the green.

It drove these strange new limbs onward, this muscle, this meat, propelling itself east, away from the fires, endeavoring to leave *Dread* behind to claim whatever world came next.

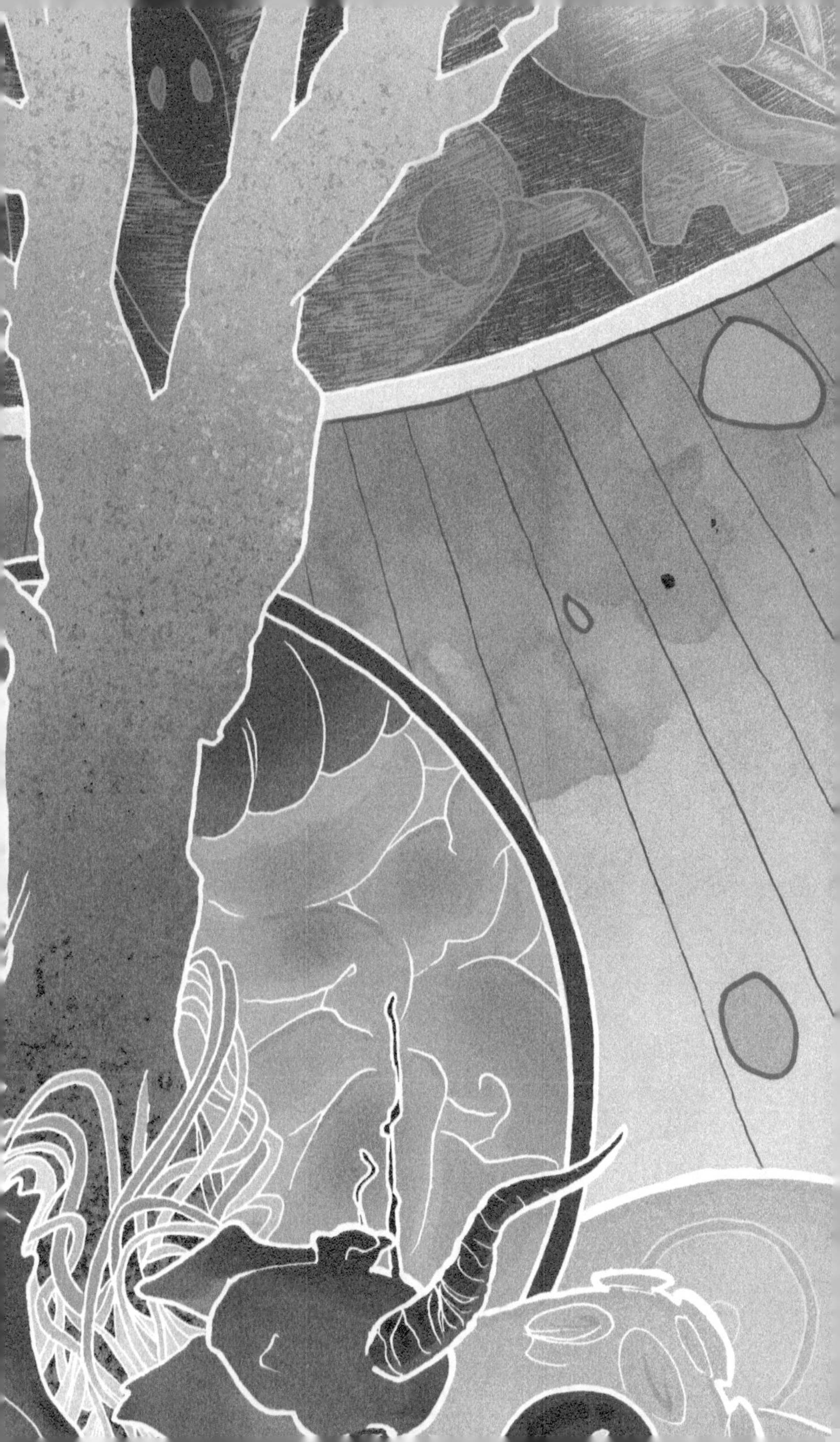

GREEN INFERNO
SNIFF

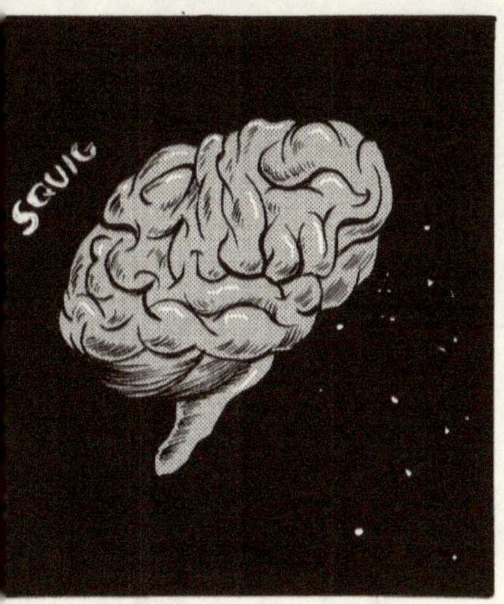

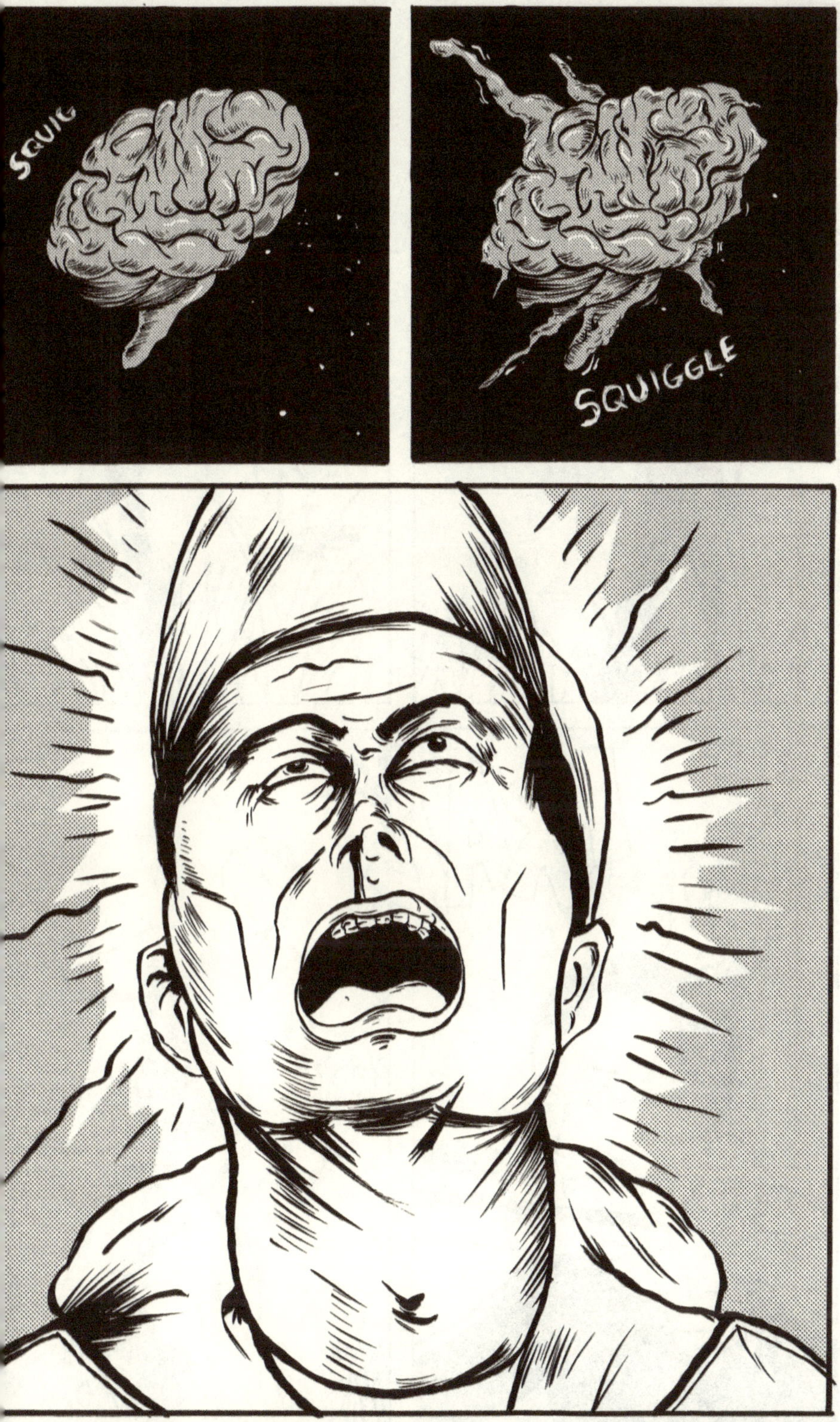

SQUIG

SQUIGGLE

KRAK

KRAK

I spent most of childhood around my grandmother...
The Romanian folk stories she'd entertain me with
tended toward the **darker side**, to put it mildly...

...Sometimes the stories are real...Seeresses
advertised in the papers and still performed
rituals to prevent the dead from rising--
at least they did as of twenty years ago...
digging up graves of suspected Strigoi,
driving nails through their skulls....

Alex Woodroe

DEPTH OF THE WATER

...But it's not all spooky castles and bloodsucking
barons...It's about daily life, embracing nature,
shining a light into the darkness...That's what
I wish for the future: that my people take back
our culture and show everyone our stories have
far more nuance and depth than they realise...

...the world celebrates our demise, not because
it wants us gone, but because IT TRIED
SO HARD TO SAVE US AND WE DID
OUR VERY BEST TO GET IN ITS WAY...

DEPTH OF THE WATER
BY ALEX WOODROE

"That dog has gills."

"Ayup."

The porch creaked when I leaned closer to my old buddy, Vernon. "Should we talk to her about it?"

"Nah." He took a swig of beer and left the bottle on my bannister before heading back in next door. I emptied mine in the magnolia bush. The way things were going, it was probably time to quit, anyway.

***

I only lasted about half a day. Talking to her wasn't high on my list of likes, either, but we had to know. Two years ago, just before the meteor hit, all the wild game took off. We didn't even think it was weird; animals always know things we don't. Six houses got knocked flat, though, and she was out there taking notes.

Last year, all the pets suddenly became burrowers the week before that sandstorm rolled in. By then, I was sure she must have had a hand in it. We survived by hunkering down in wine cellars and cowering in bathtubs. Gills, though? Gills were worse.

Her house was just a few down. Pumpkins and plastic skeletons decorated her front lawn, not a care in the world that it was the middle of August. She kept putting the damned things up earlier and earlier each year. The first time I'd knocked on her door, I admit, the pop-up Dracula with realistic blood splatter scared the daylights out of me. This time, I only jumped a little.

There was no answer. I thought I heard some shuffling inside, but nothing after that. I went back home and cracked open a beer.

***

Half the cats in the neighborhood waddled in the pond, teaching the kittens how to use their new webbed paws.

Anxiety was one thing, but we were whipped up into a full-on frothy panic. Some of the neighbors packed up, overburdened trucks groaning as they pulled out and West. Vernon went "fishing", the coward. Twenty years of friendship, and all he had to say was *"gone fishing"* scribbled on a note. Some of us had homes we didn't want to abandon just because she couldn't keep her fingers out of Nature's business.

I knocked again, and nothing. Dust fell off the top of the doorframe. Even the Dracula was switched off. "I'm coming back with the police," I shouted at the door. It wasn't police business, and I had every intention of sorting this out myself, but I didn't want to sound like an armed lunatic.

By that evening, a dozen of us had gathered with firepower. I didn't want to say anything, but some of the guys were looking a little blue; scratching at scabs behind their ears and itching their tailbones. Everyone was breathing heavy; even me. One of the guys said he thought he saw a flock of low-flying birds with fins go diving and never come back up. Enough was enough. Someone had to stop her.

The cheap plywood door went down like tissue paper.

***

We found her in the attic, naked and grunting over chalk drawings like some sort of feral animal. The whole place was hung with fish bones and long, slime-covered eels. She'd strung a few around her neck, too, one's tail in the mouth of the other. You wouldn't believe the unholy stench of the place.

She seemed harmless, at first. I was at the back, so I didn't see when the first guy went down; but then she threw herself right into the middle of the group. All she did was tap Elmer on the forehead, and to the floor he went, convulsing. It was sickening to watch a big construction worker fold like that to a little woman. The others stood around in shock as she wailed, beating her chest and yelling gibberish. Maybe she was cursing us, maybe reciting her shopping list; either way, I wasn't going to let it go on.

I aimed the butt of my rifle at her mouth. She saw; started to say "You don't under—" but with one hard thrust, I cut it short.

Even unconscious, she was trouble. Caleb tried to pick her up and succumbed to violent seizures right away. Her skin was probably poison, like some sort of toad. Someone brought up bright yellow latex gloves and aprons, and I rolled her into a big old carpet. We must have looked like a gaggle of idiots, coming out of the house dressed like that, carrying the carpet between us.

If it looks stupid, but it works, it ain't stupid. She came to just as we started the fire, and it wasn't long after that she went out for good, crackling and screaming about how we got it wrong.

***

The scales on my nape were the last to fade.

We all seemed like new people by then. A lot of the pets came back, ravenous and looking for their folk. Since some families never returned, I ended up adopting myself a pup; named him Vernon. That jerk was still gone. I worried maybe he was too far away and didn't get cured. Maybe he was slopping around in a mud puddle somewhere, breathing the filth.

New Vernon didn't like beer, but he still hung out on the porch with me, and that was good enough.

He was one of the first to spot it. The fur down his back stood up and he growled a little puppy growl. I looked where he was pointing, and sure enough, there it was.

A wall of water, all the way from the bottom of the world to the top of the sky, steadily sweeping towards us.

Finally, we'd be out of Nature's way, and no witches to stop it this time.

INVERSUS III.
THE SURROGATE
...the reek of rotting fish and excrement...the click and scutter of beetles along the walls of her trachea...her own memories, or those of the Scum Queen's brethren? Vi could no longer discern...

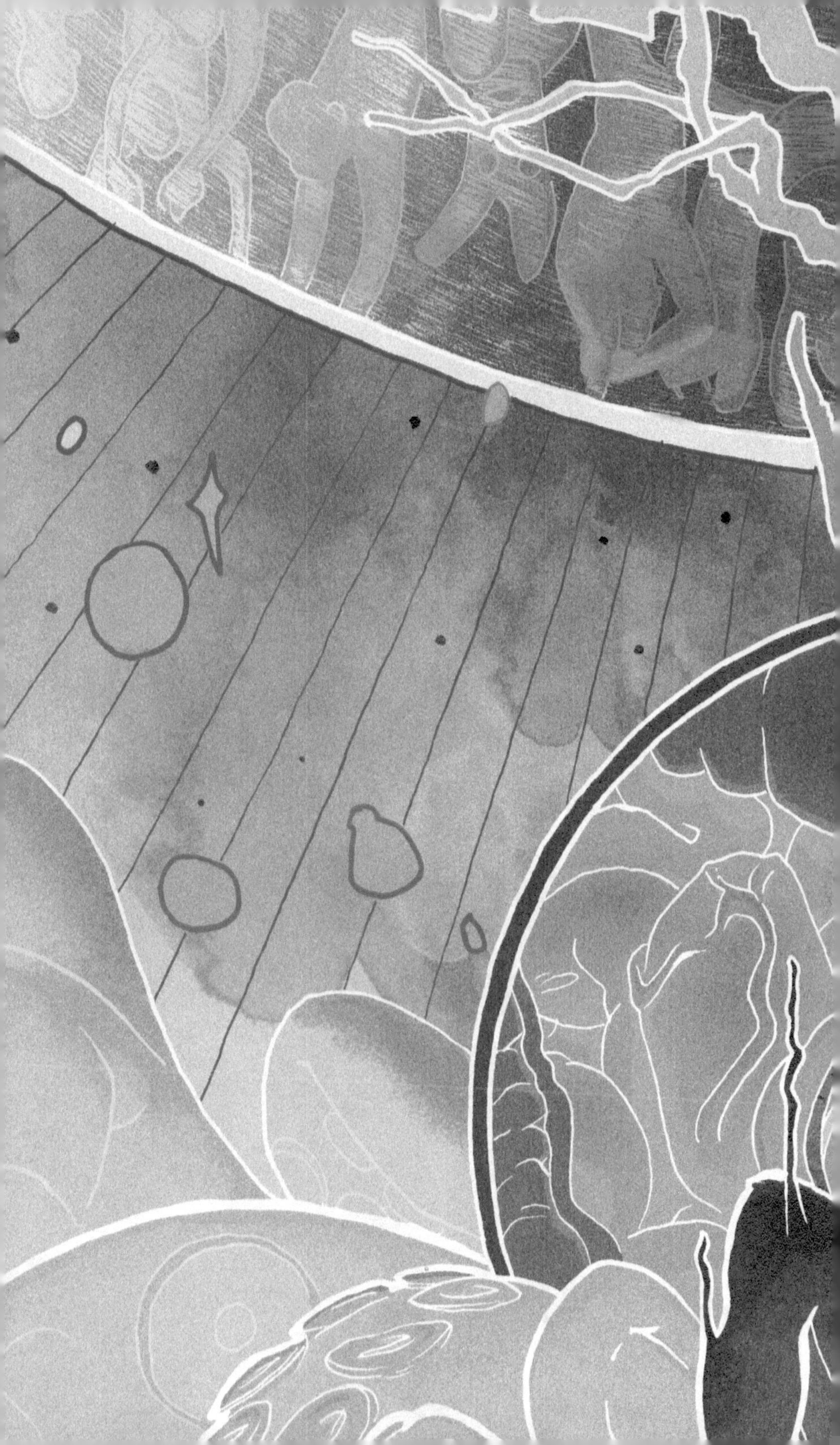

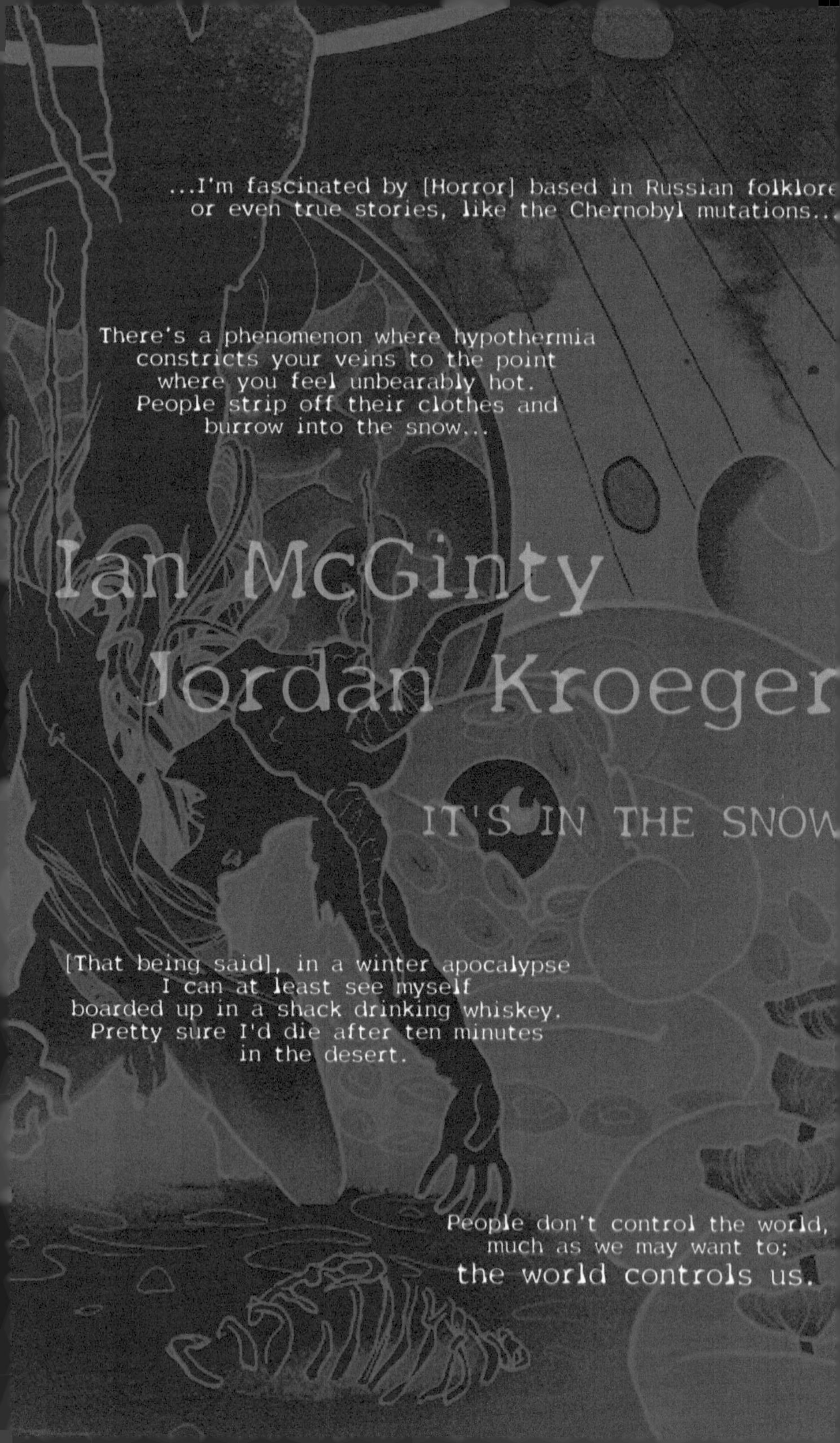

...I'm fascinated by [Horror] based in Russian folklore
or even true stories, like the Chernobyl mutations...

There's a phenomenon where hypothermia
constricts your veins to the point
where you feel unbearably hot.
People strip off their clothes and
burrow into the snow...

Ian McGinty

Jordan Kroeger

IT'S IN THE SNOW

[That being said], in a winter apocalypse
I can at least see myself
boarded up in a shack drinking whiskey.
Pretty sure I'd die after ten minutes
in the desert.

People don't control the world,
much as we may want to;
the world controls us.

IT'S IN THE SNOW

Written by IAN McGINTY   Illustrated by JORDAN KROEGER

HA! I ENDURE SOFIA! JUST YESTERDAY SHE ASKED ME WHY WE DON'T JUST HEAD BACK HOME.
I SAID, WHAT DO WE HAVE LEFT THERE, WOMAN? HERE, IT'S GLORIOUS!
FRESH AIR! GAME! FISH! A MAN COULDN'T ASK FOR ANYTHING ELSE, EH, ALEX?
POOMF
AH, MAKSIM!
SEE, THIS IS WHAT YOU GET!
YOU LITERALLY STEPPED YOUR FOOT IN IT!
MAKSIM, LET'S GET BACK TO OUR FRIENDS, YEAH?

GRAAHHH!

SOFIA, PLEASE, NO, I-!
DROOOOOOOOOOOOM

PLOP
PLOP
PLOP
PLOP

...MAKSIM...?

ANNIKA! LELYAH! DIMITRI!
IT'S IN THE SNOW!
IT'S IN THE SNOW!
IT'S IN THE SNOW!
ALEX?
PAPA?

DROOOOOOOOOOOM

ANNIKA...?

...DIMITRI?

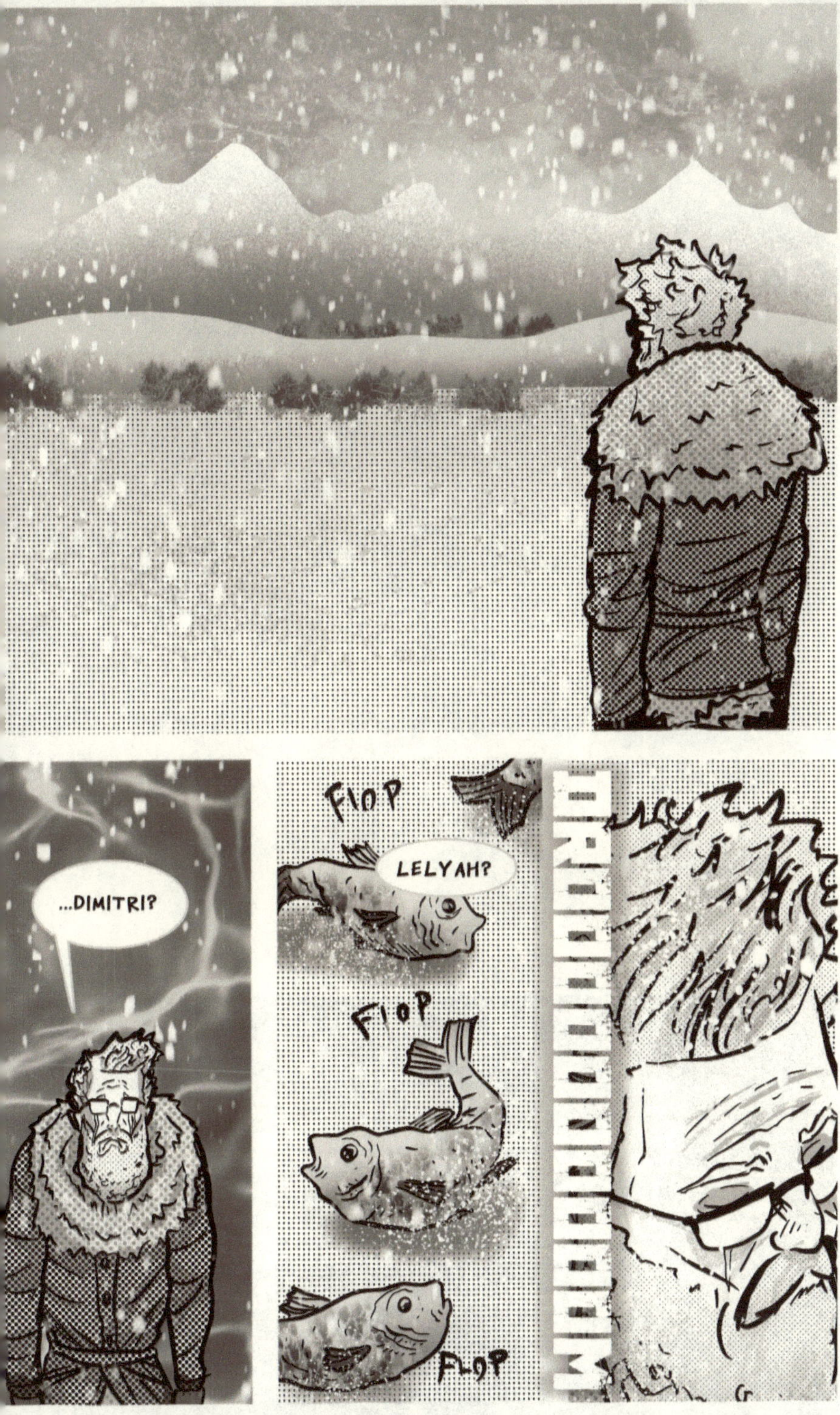

FLOP
LELYAH?
FLOP
FLOP

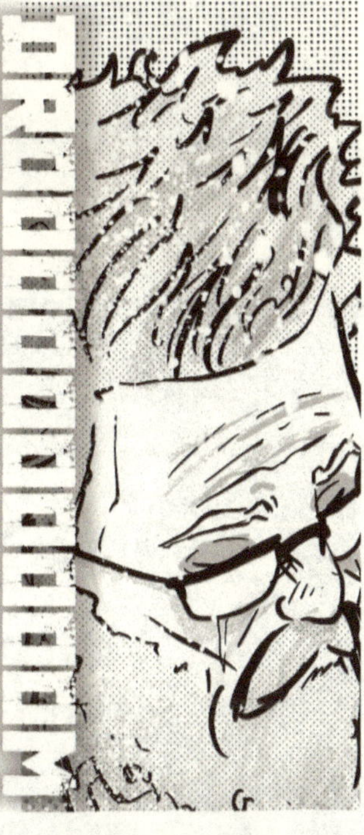
DRRRRRRRRRMM

The bodies of Alexander, Maksim and the ████████ Party
were never recovered, though au-thorities did discover
their mostly intact camp site.

A Geiger counter picked up trace amounts of radiation,
of which has never been fully understood.

To this day the mystery of the snow remains.

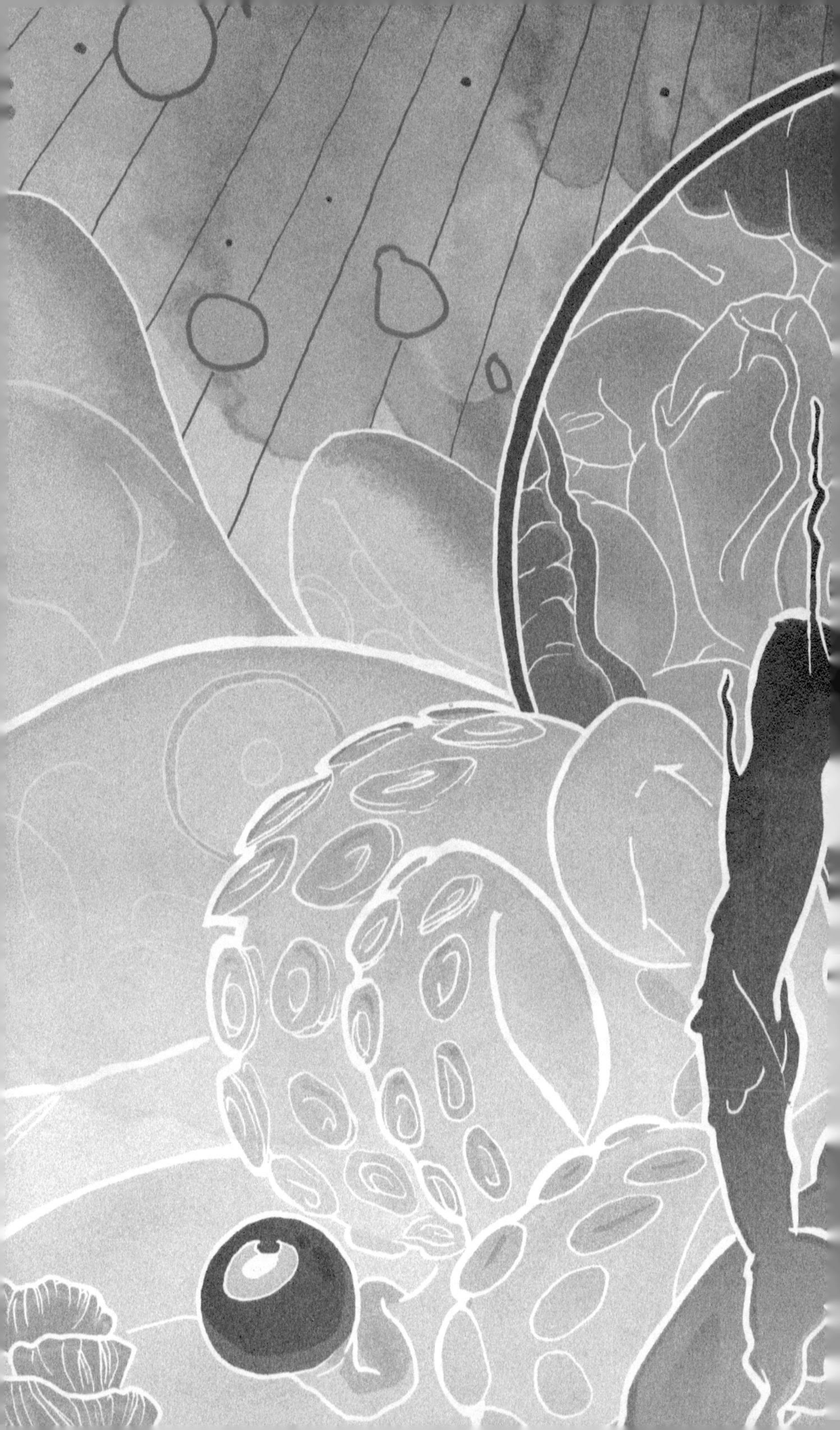

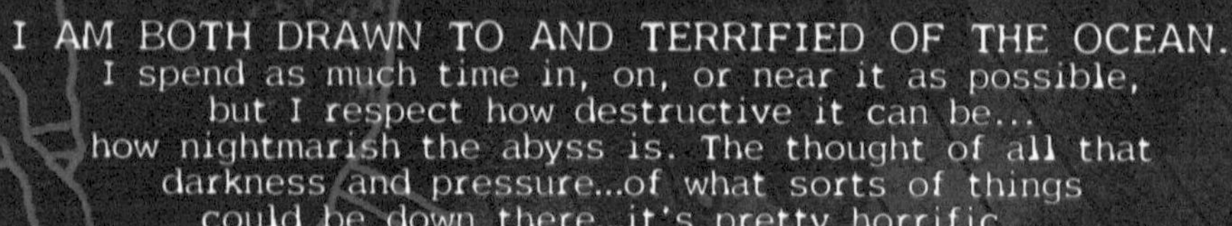

I AM BOTH DRAWN TO AND TERRIFIED OF THE OCEAN.
I spend as much time in, on, or near it as possible,
but I respect how destructive it can be...
how nightmarish the abyss is. The thought of all that
darkness and pressure...of what sorts of things
could be down there...it's pretty horrific...

Marc Sorondo

THE ROPE

...I have five kids; people often ask how I
have time to write! They're great inspiration...
Fatherhood has definitely changed my writing...
slowed it down, but [it's] also made it better...

"The Rope" fits the premise, The World
Celebrates Your Demise, [by exploring] the way
the natural rules are bent to ensure said demise...
What should be an exciting thing gets twisted
into something horrible, in large part because
NATURE STOPS PLAYING BY THE RULES.

THE ROPE
BY MARC SORONDO

Even in their earliest memories, Doug and Ken recalled the rope. It was its sheer distance from the shore that had first captured their attention and imagination. It had seemed an impossible distance to boys not yet able to swim. It floated out there, held up by the occasional faded buoy, and tempted them.

Someday, they decided early on...*someday* they would swim out to it. They would cross that vast distance and feel its coarse fibers with their pruny fingers. They would cling to it and look back to their parents on the shore and marvel at what they'd done.

It was, they assured themselves and each other, simply a matter of time.

***

The Rope

They learned to swim in summers on the island. Doug had taken to it like a fish, but Ken had spluttered and splashed his way through several vacations building his stamina and developing a smooth stroke that let him cut through the water like a seal.

Doug had been ready, but he'd waited the few years for his cousin to catch up. They'd vowed to swim out to the rope together, and together was how they would do it.

***

Doug let out a breathless cry of exhilaration as he tightened his grip around the rough cords and pulled himself close to it.

Finally. The word echoed in his mind as he listened to the splashing of Ken's approach. *Finally.* It was a cry of victory and a prayer of thanks combined.

The rope rubbed against his chest; his arms were slung over it. There was a slickness to it, a mildew slime between the abrasive fibers. It was unpleasant, but he hung there, his feet dangling over the deep, ignoring the feeling as he caught his breath.

There was a jerk that pulled him through the water as Ken grabbed the rope and hauled himself close to it.

Doug put a hand to his shoulder. "We did it," he said.

Ken panted and nodded. "We did."

***

For a few minutes they hung there, suspended in the water, rising

186

and falling with each gentle swell that passed. They breathed until the rhythm of their respiration slowed, letting the ache fade from their shoulders, arms, legs.

Doug bobbed on the surface, eyes closed, the sun warm on his back, enjoying the caress of the water's faint currents.

Then Ken asked, "Where's the shore?" and Doug's eyes snapped open.

He took the rope in his hands and turned himself. There was endless ocean behind them. Doug shrugged and said, "It's like an illusion. A mirage or something."

"That doesn't make sense."

"I don't know how mirages work," Doug said. "Do you?"

"It's something to do with heat on the ground."

"Okay. It's hot today. That's making a mirage so we can't see the shore."

Ken didn't say anything.

"We just swam here," Doug said. "We know it's there. Rest for another minute and then we'll swim back."

Ken nodded, but his gaze never left that point on the horizon where the shore should have been.

***

Doug peered down into the water. He could not see the bottom; it darkened to black beneath them.

A chill ran up his spine. Anything could be down there, waiting in that gloom. His mind conjured images of gigantic sharks with toothy maws agape and huge squid with writhing tentacles and snapping beaks. Another thought occurred to him, one that was worse in a way he did not understand: *nothing* was beneath them…nothing but the cold, crushing abyss.

It was always night down there…always winter.

Doug pulled his eyes from the depths. "Ready to go?"

***

He heard it through his own splashing: "Stop! Doug, stop!" He did so and turned to find Ken a few yards back, gasping and treading water.

Doug turned and looked back. There was no shore.

"We've gone too far. It wasn't this far when we swam out," Ken said.

Doug knew that was true.

"We have to go back to the rope," Ken said.

"Can you make it?"

Ken nodded. "It's that or drown." He turned back and swam hard.

Doug squinted into the distance. He didn't see the rope. If that had gone now too…Ken was right: it was the rope or drown.

He took a deep breath and followed. He swam hard to catch up and matched his cousin's speed once beside him.

***

They'd reached the rope—shoulder's burning, arms heavy as lead—and clung to it, gasping. Then they'd screamed themselves hoarse, praying that sound could travel a distance that had become impossible to traverse or understand.

They fell quiet as the sun crept towards the horizon, sending out orange brilliance that turned water and sky the same hue.

"What are we going to do?" Ken asked.

Doug shook his head. "I don't know." A moment later he turned and pointed to where the shore should have been. "They'll come looking for us. Maybe they already are."

"But where the hell are we?"

Doug shook his head again. "I don't know, but they'll find us. We just have to hang on until they get here."

Sea and sky became pink.

Doug thought about the fading light and the dark that would follow…a dark to mirror the night that waited in the depths beneath them… he considered the deep and said a silent prayer that help would come before the sun had set.

***

The brilliance of dawn reflected on the water roused them. After long hours on the surface of the dark, exhaustion had overcome them.

When they woke, they were draped over the rope, the sides of their faces submerged, the circulation to their arms all but cut off.

Ken let out a long, creaking groan. "I'd hoped it was a dream." His voice was hoarse. He'd do no more screaming for a while.

Doug turned and looked back toward shore but found a uniformity of gentle swells reflecting the light of dawn for as far as he could see. At least the sun had returned to keep the black water at a distance.

"What are we going to do?" Ken asked.

"Keep waiting," Doug said. "It's all we can do."

***

Their skin had taken on shades neither boy would have thought possible. The sun had burned them pink, then fiery red, and then—after several unprotected hours—a sick, purplish color.

Doug wondered what came after their skin blistered. What did a burn further roasted in the sun become? He turned to Ken and, upon seeing the expression on his cousin's face, realized that such a thought was better kept to himself.

Ken's expression combined weariness with a terror that loomed just beneath the surface. He was going to lose it soon.

"Forget it," Doug said.

Ken turned to him as if Doug had called his name.

"Forget waiting. We need to do something." Doug shook his head. "I'm not just going to float here and burn."

Ken nodded. The idea that they would take some action, undefined though it were, did him some good.

"What should we do?"

Doug looked around. He had nothing to work with but the rope itself.

"Okay," he said. "Rope's got to be tied to something, right?"

Ken looked down the length of the rope, first north and then south. "I would have thought so, but…,the beach is gone."

"I can't explain that, but..." Doug gave the rope a tug. "It's stretched taut. It's not just floating around."

Ken took the rope in both hands. He pulled with his left hand and pushed with his right and the rope curved slightly. He studied this curve for a moment. "But I don't see anything," he said when he looked up.

"Neither do I," Doug said. "So what. That just means it's not close." He pointed north. "If we follow the rope, we'll get to an end. It might take a long time, but we've got nothing better to do."

Ken nodded. "Let's go."

Doug started, pulling himself hand over hand along the rope. He looked back after a few feet and saw the look on Ken's face: terror still, but determination as well.

***

Sun burns burnt further blistered. Burned blisters burst and oozed before crusting over in spite of the salt water.

There was no escape from the sun: not a cloud in the sky to obscure it for even a moment, nor a shadow in all the world to hide beneath.

They dragged themselves through the sea for hours before Ken stopped.

"Doug."

Doug kept going, so focused on the rhythm of pulling that he was all but deaf.

"Doug!"

Doug stopped and turned back.

"This is pointless."

Doug looked past Ken, then turned to look farther down the rope. Water. Nothing but water.

"We've been going all day. I'm tired, and I'm thirsty, and we're not getting anywhere."

Doug nodded. "It just keeps going."

"What happened to us?"

Doug shook his head. He couldn't understand the omnipresence of water. He couldn't find words of hope, or even a half-hearted suggestion. "I don't know."

***

That night the fevers came. They'd been burned sick by the sun and the water was ice cold.

Their shivering—violent enough to keep them awake most of the night—splashed and sent ripples back and forth in the water between them.

The moon was an orb on the surface and a shimmer on the edge of every ripple; but below, the blackness waited.

***

The sun banished the darkness to the depths, but it burned.

They bobbed cold and weak in the water, their dry mouths mocked by the water around them, their ruined flesh roasted.

Blisters that had burst, that had cracked and crusted over, now bled. There were pink auras draped around their shoulders.

"We're going to die out here," Ken said. He was holding on with his left hand and swishing his right through the faint cloud of blood, watching it swirl and fade as it passed through his fingers.

"No, we're not," Doug said.

Ken's hand went still, hovering just below the water's surface. "There is no shore."

Doug considered this. He wanted to argue…but they'd gone so far only to flee back to the rope; they'd climbed along the rope for hours and what must have been miles and nothing but more rope had greeted them.

He couldn't argue.

There was no shore.

***

Ken saw the fins first.

With a calm that Doug found unsettling, he reached over and tapped Doug on his burnt forearm.

"Look," he said, nodding at the fin that cut through the water in a wide arc around them.

Doug sighed. "We're bleeding. We're bleeding into the water."

"Nothing we can do," Ken said.

Another fin broke the surface.

"They say to hit a shark in the eye, right? That'll make them leave you alone?" Doug asked.

Ken shrugged. "I don't know if that's true."

"Of course it's true. *Nothing* likes getting hit in the eye."

A third fin rose. Sleek forms circled through the water, long grey bodies moving with slow strokes of powerful tails. Each was as long as both boys together.

One shark built speed and darted in, before moving past them and back out to resume circling.

Another came too close and Doug lashed out, missing its eye and jabbing the side of its head instead.

The big fish veered off and made a wider loop for a few rotations before rejoining the narrowing ring of water occupied by the others.

Doug kept the fingers of his right hand bent into talons, his head turning as he tried—and failed—to watch all three sharks at once.

Ken held the rope with both hands, looking back toward where the shore should have been. The sharks passed in front of him, but he didn't watch them go by.

There was a strange sensation. Doug was floating higher in the water, lifted by pressure from below, by the force of something enormous rising from the black depths.

He looked down. The gloom had risen. It was night just below their feet.

The sharks darted away, scattering and sending up splashes with their tails in their desperation to flee.

Doug watched as the night receded. In seconds it looked normal beneath them.

***

Doug didn't recognize the sounds that had woken him at first. He opened his eyes and squinted at the reflection of the morning sun on the water.

For an instant sky and surface looked identical. He could not orient himself until he tightened his grip on the rope. Grounded, he could tell which way was up.

He rubbed at his eyes and wondered if dehydration had caused his confusion or if—like the shore—the separation between sea and sky was being stolen from them a little bit at a time.

He looked around, seeking the noise that had disturbed him.

Ken was gone.

His shock roused him enough to recognize the sound of weak splashing that gave away Ken's position. His cousin was swimming, going as hard as he could in a straight line, headed to where the beach should have been.

"Ken!" Doug's voice was weak. He tried to moisten his mouth with spit and found that he couldn't. "Kenny!"

If Ken heard him at all, he didn't react.

Doug pushed off from the rope.

Ken had a substantial lead, but Doug knew he was faster; he knew that, over the endless ocean, he had plenty of time to catch up.

Doug hadn't had anything to eat or drink in days. His body would not cooperate, but he'd practiced so hard for so long that swimming was like reflex. He moved through the water, his strokes smooth and efficient, his exhausted legs kicking up spray and propelling him forward.

He interrupted his rhythm to look ahead. Ken was still far away, but Doug was closing the distance.

He swam on. Doug tried to kill the seed of hope that began to sprout within him—*Ken must have seen something; this would be the end of their ordeal.*

He knew the truth. There was no shore, no rescue. There was only the rope…and the black deep.

Hope had no place there.

Doug swam harder. He had to catch his cousin before they got too far from the rope to make it back.

The leathery, burnt skin of his shoulders stung. It cracked and bled. He pictured a comet trail of pink water behind him, but he ignored it and swam.

He slowed and looked up again. Ken was gone.

"Kenny!" Doug waited a beat, his speed slowed to all but a stop. "Kenny!"

Doug stuck his face in the water and forced his eyes open against the sting of the salt. Deep in the water ahead of him, Ken's motionless body sank.

Doug lifted his head, took a deep breath, and dove. He swam at a forty-five degree angle. The building pressure made his head pound. His lungs ached.

He kept his burning eyes open and locked on Ken's body…until something else moved.

The gloom rose up from the depths, pushing water ahead of it. Inky black, as if a cup of liquid midnight had been poured into morning ocean; it rose and spread.

Doug swam harder, forcing himself against the rising wave of pressure. His ears felt like they would burst, his eyes like they would pop from their sockets.

The darkness enveloped Ken's body slowly, the way a cloud moved in the sky on a spring afternoon.

Doug neared. He reached out, propelling himself with his kicking feet. His fingers were inches from the inky cloud. Ken's body, obscured but still visible, was just beneath.

Then, in a single, violent motion, Ken's body was pulled into the deep.

Doug screamed into the abyss, emptied his lungs and felt the true power of the crushing weight of water.

He closed his eyes and kicked hard for the surface. Once he looked down, expecting to see the darkness rising in pursuit. Instead it settled back in place.

Doug kicked and fought the urge to inhale. He flapped his arms as if imitating a bird, desperate to pull himself up, to reach the surface and breathe. His ears popped. His chest spasmed, trying to fill his lungs with salt water, but he refused it.

He broke the surface and inhaled a huge, ragged breath that felt like fire and salvation. He took several more, relishing the pain.

Ken was gone. He was alone now.

Worse…he wasn't.

***

He swam with his eyes closed. He blocked out everything but the rhythm of swimming. He'd come to believe that he must have gone in the wrong direction. He'd gotten far enough chasing Ken that being off by just a few degrees meant he'd never make it back to the rope.

He swam with his eyes closed, repeating the word *swim* again and again in his mind. He'd swim until he died. He didn't care how his muscles ached. He'd swim until he died on the surface with the sun shining down on him.

The darkness couldn't have him.

Then, as he brought his arm back into the water, something caught his forearm and ruined his rhythm.

He recoiled instinctively and opened his eyes.

The rope was stretched out to infinity across his path.

Doug grabbed it with both hands and pulled himself to it. It felt rough under his arms and against his chest. It smelled of rot and mold. He closed his eyes again and focused on the sensation of rough fibers against his sunburnt skin.

In a liquid world, it alone was tangible. Everything else slipped away, but the rope remained.

Doug turned his head and lowered it until half his face was under water. He could breathe through the side of his mouth as if he were still swimming. He fell asleep that way, as if frozen mid-stroke.

***

It was dark when he woke.

That was the worst. Though the night offered relief from the sun, it also changed the character of the sea. The water was black from the surface to the deepest trench. At night, it was all abyss.

Doug's body ached, though differently than when he'd swam himself to the point of exhaustion getting back to the rope. He was conscious of his own heartbeat. It felt strong…but labored, as if it took his body more work than it should to make it throb.

A moon hung in the sky; another floated on the water's surface.

In the distance, where land should have been, there was only black water.

Doug squeezed the rope with both hands. Nothing else was real.

Then he pushed himself away from it.

He swam for the beach at a leisurely pace. There would be no frantic race for a shore he'd never reach. He was beyond blind panic now… beyond illusions of hope.

He'd die with some dignity.

He swam and the soreness of his muscles and his leathery, cracked skin felt distant, as if he'd left it dangling from the rope.

He knew he'd never swim back into that other world; he'd never see the faces or hear the voices of his mother or father or anyone else ever again. It was over, everything but the last bit of it, and he could accept that as long as he did that last bit his way.

Then he felt it, like he was floating higher on the water. He moved over a swell displaced by the rising of something enormous from the deep.

Doug swam faster. He refused the rising depths. The night could not have him.

The approaching horror created in him a hope he did not want, one that his weary mind could not believe. He refused the abyss. He would swim into the morning of another world even if he had to swim forever.

The night would not have him.

Doug swam with furious energy born of defiance. He felt no pain now; he was not tired. He'd left those concerns at the rope. Now he had only to swim…to swim into the light of dawn.

The blackness rose and embraced him. The night water slipped around him, passed over him and caressed him. It moved like a cloud and it felt like chilled velvet.

Doug's pace slowed. The abyss held him. It moved with him and he moved with it.

He descended into the crushing unknown of eternal night, his pace unhurried, his destination unreachable.

***

There was only the rope, its faded yellow chords braided together, fraying tufts of ruined fibers here and there, the stench of mold and decay clinging to it. It stretched out into eternity in either direction.

GREEN INFERNO

MARSHA

AND JOHN'S HERE TOO!

I'M SO HAPPY WE'RE ALL TOGETHER AGAIN

INVERSUS IV.
GATECRASH

The transmission from PROJECT: PLUTO was brief and impossible to misinterpret...

FAILURE TO CONTAIN.

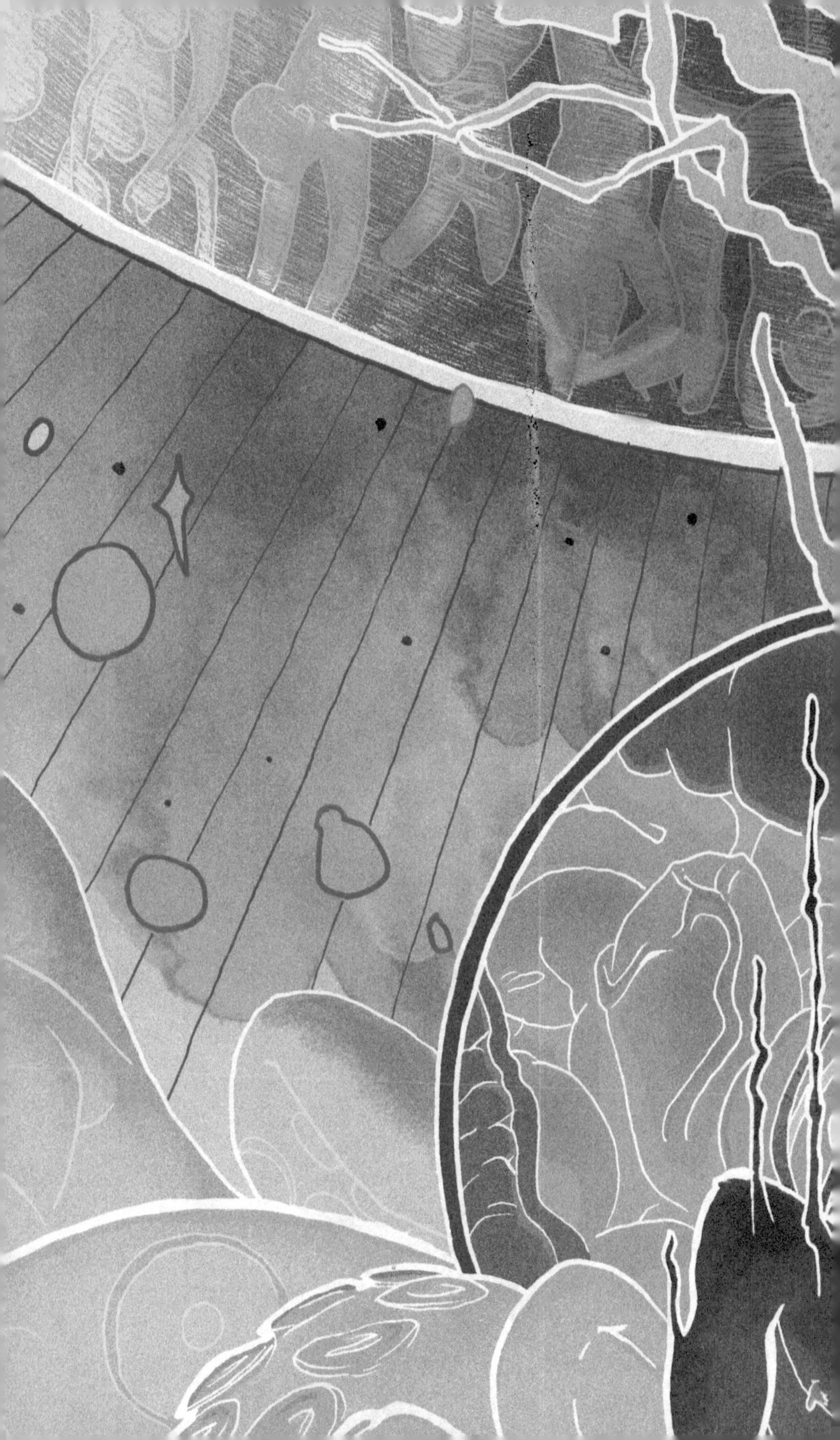

Kristofor Harris

GREEN INFERNO cover artist

I'm kind of all over the place with my favorite [Horror].
I really love stories that don't just focus on cheap thrill
and spectacle but tell interesting stories with cool characters.
As an artist I'm always focused on the artwork,
but if you have a cool premise and execution, I'm in.

Art is my hobby as well as my profession.
I love [exploring] new mediums.
I tend to burn the candle at both ends,
but I'm always exploring ways to get
better and hone my craft. I have a soft spot for
Spanish/Mexican/South American artists,
and I've been diving head first into
finding great stories they're telling.

I always try to stay positive, but I encourage everyone to find
something creative to do. Write a poem, draw a doodle, make a
movie, whatever you can do to siphon those hard feelings and
**find some respite in this big weird
world we are living in right now.**

GREEN INFERNO ALUMNI

Diane Barker is a bisexual queer lady. She hails from England but now resides in beautiful Portland, Oregon. She writes horror tales and stories with heart, and has contributed to several anthologies. Diane enjoys inhaling chai lattes and tasty bagels, helping her friends table at conventions, and sipping whiskey on the patio.

Bobby Bermea is a multi-disciplinary artist with a lifelong passion for speculative fiction and art. Writer, director, performer, Bermea seeks to answer the muse in whatever medium she chooses to contact him through.

Matt Blairstone (he/him) is a Horror writer and indie comics creator. He is solely to blame for the psychedelic/absurdist/sci-fi comics series *Mad Doctors*; its latest volume, *Mondo Cosmico: Regret Nothing,* is out now. In addition, Matt is the publisher for Tenebrous Press and editor for *Green Inferno.* He lives in Portland, Oregon with wife (and fellow artist) Kate Blairstone and their four-year-old terror who walks like a boy.

Michael Falotico is an illustrator and musician born and raised in New York City. Striking a balance between hyper minimalism and intricate detail, Falotico presents unsettling scenarios and strange characters we can all relate to. When he isn't drawing, Michael can be found playing the bass guitar or staring deeply into the wall.

Kristofor Harris is an artist out of Kansas City, currently working on his creator-owned series, *Ancient Cosmonauts,* and numerous other projects.

Toshiya Kamei holds an MFA in literary translation from the University of Arkansas. His translations of short fiction and poetry have appeared in venues such as *Abyss & Apex, Cosmic Roots & Eldritch Shores, The Magazine of Fantasy & Science Fiction, Samovar,* and *Star*Line.*

Umiyuri Katsuyama is a Japanese writer of fantasy and horror. In 2011, she won the Japan Fantasy Novel Award with her novel *Sazanami no kuni.* Her most recent novel, *Chuushi, ayashii nabe to tabi wo suru,* was published in 2018. Her short fiction has appeared in numerous horror anthologies in Japan.

Lorna D. Keach (she/her) lives and writes in Omaha, Nebraska, US. Her work has appeared in various small print and online publications over the years, but she recently took off time from publishing to have a baby, hone her craft, read some books, summon a few friendly demons, etc. etc. She would love it if you popped in and said hi at lornakeach.com.

Spencer Koelle haunts a Philadelphia row house with his partner and two orange cats. He mixes cocktails, worships Pagan idols, and watches horror movies on DVD. His website is spencerkoelle.com, his twitter is @KoelleSpencer, and his blood is hot.

Jordan Kroeger is a Kansas City comic creator currently serializing *TIGER-BOY VERSUS* on Patreon.

Michelle Lodge is an illustrator and comic artist whose signature styles include both stark B&W noir and comedically cartoonish. She has drawn the comic series *The Black Wall* and the all ages series *Whiz Bang the Boy Robot,* as well as the semi-autobiographical webcomic strip *Moementality*. Follow her on Twitter, Instagram and Facebook.

Ian McGinty is an American comic book writer and artist known for his work on *Adventure Time, Bee and PuppyCat* and *Invader Zim.* He is best known for his creator owned comic *Welcome to Showside.*

Eric Neher is an award-winning author who resides in Newcastle Oklahoma. His notable published works include *Permian Remorse, The Cycle, A Fractured Frame,* and many others. His novel *The Killing Pledge* is due to be released in June 2021.

Lena Ng shambles around Toronto, Ontario as a zombie member of the Horror Writers Association. She gnaws brains at night, when no one knows she's awake. She has written for over four dozen publications, including *Amazing Stories, Twisted Love, What Monsters Do for Love, Hybrid Fiction, The London Reader* and *Tales from the Moonlit Path*. "Under an Autumn Moon" is her short story collection. She is currently seeking a publisher for her Gothic romance novel, *Darkness Beckons*.

Harry Nordlinger is a cartoonist/artist/illustrator from San Francisco, specializing in absurdity, surreal horror and the macabre. He is known for the self-published comic book anthologies *Softer Than Sunshine* and *Vacuum Decay*.

Erica Ruppert writes Weird fiction and poetry from her home in northern New Jersey. Her work has appeared in *PodCastle*, *Lamplight Magazine* and *Nightmare*, among others. Her novella, *Sisters in Arms,* will be released by Trepidatio Publishing in the summer of 2021.

Blacky Shepherd is a Pacific Northwest-based comic book artist and writer, best known for his horror collaborations with Cullen Bunn. He's also done work on *G.I. Joe* and *The Transformers* for IDW Comics, and is currently working on a boutique toy line based on his original characters.

Marc Sorondo lives with his wife and children in New York. He loves to read, and his interests range from fiction to comic books, physics to history, oceanography to cryptozoology, and just about everything in between. He's a perpetual student and occasional teacher. For more information, go to MarcSorondo.com.

Harrison Webb is a geeky, queer, horror-loving illustrator based in Portland, Oregon, and the face behind Fiendish Thingy Art. His art balances creepy and cute and often touches on the mythical in the process. He recently received his MFA in Visual Development and uses his skills in watercolour, ink, and digital media to create character and creature designs, comics and more.

Alex Woodroe was raised—possibly by wolves—in Romania, on the outskirts of Transylvania. She found her way into weird, transgressive fiction through a gateway in the woods and made a career out of doing terrible things to words in multiple languages. Her favourite horror story is *Alice in Wonderland.* She is a member of the Horror Writers Association. You can chat with her on Twitter @ AlexWoodroe or at woodroewriting.com

ABOUT TENEBROUS PRESS

Tenebrous Press was conceived in the Plague Year 2020 and unleashed, howling and feral, in spring 2021 to deliver the finest in *transgressive, progressive Horror prose and comics* from diverse and unsung voices around the world.

We welcome the esoteric; the unorthodox; the Weirdest of Weird Fiction and Horror.

FIND OUT MORE:

www.tenebrouspress.com

Twitter: @TenebrousPress

HAIL INDIE HORROR.